THE TRAIL WAS CUT!

The horses stood, ears pricked, sniffing the breeze. Mike moved clear of them. Then he caught it, too. Smoke!

"What's wrong?" Calhoun asked.

"Trouble ahead. Let's look."

They cat-footed ahead in the darkness. They came to a drop-off. Down below, fire formed a crimson pool. A building was burning. They could make out a stagecoach; then it, too, began to burn. Figures moved in the firelight, a tortured screaming came to their ears. The air bore the acrid, terrifying smell of burning flesh!

And then a shrill yelping arose that might have come from animals. But these were not animals—

THEY WERE APACHES!

Books by Cliff Farrell

FOLLOW THE NEW GRASS

WEST WITH THE MISSOURI

SANTA FE WAGON BOSS

RIDE THE WILD TRAIL

THE LEAN RIDER

FORT DECEPTION

Published by Bantam Books

TRAIL OF THE
TATTERED STAR
CLIFF FARRELL

A HISTORICAL NOVEL OF THE WEST

*This low-priced Bantam Book
has been completely reset in a type face
designed for easy reading, and was printed
from new plates. It contains the complete
text of the original hard-cover edition.*
NOT ONE WORD HAS BEEN OMITTED.

TRAIL OF THE TATTERED STAR

*A Bantam Book / published by arrangement with
Doubleday & Company, Inc.*

PRINTING HISTORY
*Doubleday edition published December 1961
Bantam edition published February 1964*

*Bantam Books are published by Bantam Books, Inc. Its trade-mark,
consisting of the words "Bantam Books" and the portrayal of a
bantam, is registered in the United States Patent Office and in other
countries. Marca Registrada. Printed in the United States of America. Bantam Books, Inc., 271 Madison Ave., New York 16, N. Y.*

CHAPTER ONE

After those months on the barren ribs of the continental divide this was heaven. This was feast and Mike McLish forgot the famine. He drew the breeze off the Pacific into his lungs, marveling at its briny coolness.

He lifted his hat to a comely young lady who passed by in a carriage. She tilted her nose to snub him, then took a second look and gazed back a trifle wistfully as the vehicle carried her away from him forever.

He strolled onward along the sidewalk past polished gentlemen, past horse-smelling *vaqueros* from the ranchos, past traders in broadcloth and beggars in rags, past miners in red shirts and kept women in furs. Coolies in round hats from the Yangtze walked in the mud along with mules and horses and with "Sydney ducks" whose ears had been bobbed in Australian convict colonies. Past all the panoply of feverish San Francisco on this February day in 1861.

All of this bubbled in Mike's blood like champagne. He would have traded places with no person on earth at this moment. He wanted to sing and dance and match wits with a pretty girl and tell her tall stories she would pretend to believe.

He twirled a walking stick. He had never before carried one. Even yesterday he would have scorned the thought of such an affectation. Today it was in keeping with his spirit.

He wore a fashionable knee-length coat with square pearl buttons. Its color was pearl gray. A cloth hat to match was tilted on his dark hair. His trousers were a rich cinnamon hue, his waistcoat was of watered silk, with a satin cravat snugged against a ruffled linen shirt. His boots were new and as soft as suede.

All this had cost a pretty penny. He jingled gold coins in his pocket. Money was for the spending. In the room at the St. Nicholas Hotel were his saddle panniers containing spare clothing, a shaving kit and a few personal items. Also

1

a brace of pistols. Whatever other material possessions he had accumulated during his twenty-nine years of life were scattered among stage stations along a thousand miles of the Central Overland trail.

He paused before the window of a bank in order to inspect his reflection. He saw, with some chagrin, that his deeply tanned face was not exactly in keeping with his new city garb. His eyes, which were set beneath square black brows, seemed pale gray instead of blue against that background.

"I look like a Piute in a plug hat," he told his reflection.

He flicked lint from a lapel and set his hat at a new angle. He ran a hand over his jaws. They were razored to an unbelievable smoothness. A paid-for shave with hot towels and scented water had been luxury indeed.

He became aware of the image of another face in the glass. Its owner seemed to be peering over his shoulder. It was a feminine face and it was obviously amused.

He turned. She was an attractive young woman. She sat in a brougham which stood at the curb with a smart hackney team in harness and a coachman on the box. She must have been there all the time and Mike wondered how he could have overlooked such a fetching sight. She had slender features and her skin was very white. Her dark eyes, still amused, were big and expressive.

She continued smiling faintly as though understanding his mood, and, indeed, sharing it with him. Contrary to convention, she wore no hat but only a small wisp of white lace in the Spanish style over her dark hair. But she was not Spanish. A fur jacket was draped over her shoulders. She snugged this more closely around her, for the afternoon was waning and the usual chilly fog was drifting across the building tops and obscuring the masts of the ships in the bay. The weak sunshine had faded.

Mike removed his hat, bowed and walked toward the carriage. Her smile changed. It did not become unfriendly but it refused any undue familiarity. It also carried a sudden warning.

A man hurried from the door of the bank, brushed past Mike and swung around in front of him, blocking his path. "You're going in the wrong direction, fellow," the newcomer said.

He was tall and quietly dressed. He had arrived hatless. He had crisp brown hair which clung closely to his head. A tinge of gray at the temples might be premature, for he otherwise appeared to be about forty. His eyes were a cool shade of brown. He was handsome enough, but the bone structure of his face seemed a trifle too large for his skin, giving his jaws and chin a sharp-edged aspect.

He watched Mike with assurance as though confident of his ability at handling the situation. Mike sidestepped to his left and reversed his direction. He moved past the intruder who had been feinted into shifting out of his path and stepped to the side of the brougham.

The dark-eyed young woman had quit smiling. She was shaking her head. She was obviously alarmed.

Mike felt a hand on his shoulder. He surmised that her protector intended to whirl him around and smash a blow into his face. He ducked as he turned. He had been right. The fist that had been intended for his jaw whizzed harmlessly over his head.

The empty force of the blow carried the man forward. Mike merely stepped aside and let him be carried by his own vigor off the sidewalk. It had rained that morning and the mud was deep. The man's polished boots sank to his ankles in the mire.

He came stepping back on the sidewalk, furious. Mike braced himself for the storm, thinking regretfully of his own fine attire which, palpably, was in danger of damage.

But another man hurried from the bank and pushed between them, holding the angered one back. "Cool down, Vance!" the arrival said. "We can't be brawling with every man Julia smiles at. You'd be fighting half the male population of San Francisco. Come along."

This one had the cultured velvet of the South in his speech. His voice had depth and range. He was a man of commanding size. A mane of gray hair swept back from a strong forehead. Eyes of a stern, uncompromising shade of blue looked out from beneath shaggy brows. He wore a dark frock coat, a ruffled shirt and dark stock. A clerk rushed from the bank, handed him a silk top hat and gave his companion a cloth headpiece.

The gray-haired one evidently was accustomed to being obeyed. The younger one smoothed his ruffled feathers. He shrugged. "You're in luck, my friend," he said to Mike.

He followed his companion into the brougham and ordered the coachman to proceed. The hackneys splattered mud over bystanders as the equipage got under way. The young woman looked back at Mike. She was grave, unsmiling.

3

He was half of a mind to follow her, but no carriage was within call. The brougham was soon lost among the swarming vehicles. Mike subsided, with regret. He consulted his reflection in the window, restored his hat to the correct pitch, tucked the stick under his arm and resumed his stroll.

He continued around the plaza. He paused for a time in an ornate tavern named the El Dorado and sipped a spiced rum. The place had thick plush carpets. Carpets in a barroom! And silver cuspidors! The play at the gambling tables was noisy, the drinking heavy. The Comstock Lode in Virginia City beyond the Sierras was in bonanza silver. The Mother Lode of gold in the nearer diggings was still producing richly. San Francisco was riding high.

But beneath the glitter was great tension. A noisy dispute broke out between men at the bar. "To hell with Abe Lincoln!" one of them shouted. "Him an' all like him! To hell with the Union too, if thet's the way they want to run it. If you no'therners want a fight you'll git it for sure. There're plenty like me here in California. Ain't I right, Kirby?"

"Plenty more," the one addressed as Kirby shouted. "It won't be long before we'll have somethin' to say about joinin' the Confederacy, you mark my word."

A derisive roar arose, mingled with whoops of approval. Union supporters were in the majority in the place, but the adherents of the Confederacy formed a tight, determined group around Kirby. This man was a handsome, stalwart, blond firebrand who seemed ready to back up his views with his fists. The place boiled near the point of a free-for-all.

Mike stayed clear of it. He nursed his drink and watched the tide of debate rage. Finally it subsided, but cross-currents still ran strongly. He knew that these currents were not confined to the El Dorado. They were everywhere. In San Francisco. In California. In the nation.

He left the simmering establishment. Foggy twilight curtained the streets. He continued his stroll for another half an hour. His course was apparently aimless. He headed at times toward the wharves, and then would swing back toward the plaza. He visited another café or two but left his drinks almost untasted.

He was making certain that he was not being followed. In fact he was growing weary of the effort, for he had the thought that he was wasting time in a childish pretense at mystery.

4

Darkness came and the street lamps were pale in the fog. He looked at his watch. He would have preferred to have headed for a dining room and his supper. Instead, he strolled off the plaza along Clay Street.

Carriages lined the sidewalk. Some were for hire, with coachmen trying to buttonhole him. Others were private equipages with their drivers awaiting the return of their owners from the gambling houses.

A voice spoke from one carriage as Mike came abreast. "You are right on time, Michael."

Two men sat in the vehicle. It was a two-seated carriage, with the curtains partly in place so that the occupants were well hidden. Mike recognized the voice. He moved closer and spoke. "Hello, Mr. Majors."

A curtain was opened. "Get in, Michael," the speaker said, drawing him into the carriage.

He was barely seated before the other man, who was alone in the driver's place, sent the horses away at a trot.

"Mike," said Alexander Majors, "I want you to meet an old friend. For the time being we'll call him John Doe. You can depend on anything he has to say."

Mike briefly accepted the hand that was extended over the back of the seat. As best he could make out in the faint light of the street lamps, John Doe was a blocky-shouldered, solid-jawed man of middle age.

"Are you sure you weren't followed, McLish?" John Doe asked. He had a crisp, authoritative manner of speech.

"The note Mr. Majors left for me at the hotel told me to cover my tracks," Mike said. "I did just that."

"I'm happy to know you carry out instructions," John Doe said.

"Happy?"

"From what Alex tells me, I have the impression you are more likely to do your own thinking."

"How am I to take that?" Mike asked.

"It could be a fault under some circumstances," John Doe commented.

It was obvious that John Doe was not trusting in Mike's belief that he had not been trailed. The carriage was following a twisting course through dark streets. Both John Doe and Alexander Majors kept watching their backtrail.

Mike's impatience grew as the silence went on. "Keep your hair on, Mike," Alexander Majors said. "There's a good reason for all this skulking."

5

At last the vehicle swung into a carriageway. This led to a stable yard at the rear of a seedy house in a shabby neighborhood. The house was a frame, two-story, gabled structure. Curtains were drawn but lamplight was evident dimly both from a room below and in an upper story window.

John Doe led the way to a rear door. He listened before unlocking and opening it. He again stood listening. Satisfied, he ushered them into an unlighted kitchen.

"Wait here," he murmured.

Meals had been cooked here recently. The stove still gave forth warmth. John Doe entered the larger room. A lamp with a frosted china shade burned dimly on a sideboard. He did not turn up the wick. He opened a door which led to a stairway and spoke briefly to someone in the lighted room above. If there was an answer it was inaudible to Mike.

John Doe beckoned and they joined him in the main room. He still did not offer to brighten the light. Mike now had a better look at him. He had sandy hair and a clipped mustache and sideburns. He was a man well in his fifties, evidently. There was keen intelligence in his stern blue eyes. He wore a cheap, sack suit. Neither he nor his garb nor this shabby house seemed to match.

He spoke to Alexander Majors with some asperity. "I didn't expect such a fine-feathered individual."

Mike's patience ended. "In that case I'll drift along," he snapped. "I'll say good evening."

"He does have a strong dash of pepper in his makeup, just as you warned me, Alex." John Doe commented. "Quite a temper."

Alexander Majors seated himself in the background as though he expected to be only an onlooker. He removed his black top hat. Mike saw that he was thin and looked tired. He was the Majors of the stagecoach firm of Russell, Majors & Waddell which maintained service from Missouri to California over the Central Overland route. Central Overland was in competition with the powerful Butterfield line which operated on the long Southern Overland trail and was backed by government subsidy and mail contracts.

Central Overland had never more than met expenses. Worse yet, Russell, Majors & Waddell had taken on the monumental task of operating the fast Pony Express mail service between Sacramento and the Missouri border. Successful as far as speedy mail delivery went, the Pony Express was proving

6

to be a financial disaster. Alexander Majors, whose fortune was the backbone of his firm, faced ruin.

Majors smiled wearily. "Mike's been living with a foot in the stirrup for months. Don't let the clothes fool you. He thought he had come here for a fling. He bought himself some fancy."

Mike endured John Doe's continuing critical inspection. "Your name," John Doe said, "is Michael McLish. Scotch-Irish?"

"My mother was Irish," Mike said. "My father was Scotch. Bless their memories."

"An explosive combination," John Doe commented. He continued his survey. "You're bigger than I estimated at first. You're about six-one, I'd say. Weigh around two hundred?"

"When I'm eating regular," Mike said. "Around one ninety, mostly."

"And you're homely enough to appeal to women. They likely follow you around like sheep."

"If only that was true," Mike said.

"I note a few scars on your jaws," John Doe went on. "And a slight dent in the bridge of the nose. The souvenirs of fist fighting, I take it. Alex informs me that you also carry the marks of a bullet or two. A Cheyenne arrowhead is still buried in you somewhere."

"You seem to have me pretty well identified," Mike commented. "It's only a sliver from a war arrow. I'l have it taken out one of these days after I get settled here. It doesn't bother me much."

John Doe and Majors traded glances and smiled a little. "You may have to worry along with it for a while," John Doe said. "Alex tells me you've been valuable to him. You have a talent for stagecoaching. You surveyed and built new stretches of road for Central Overland. You helped organize the Pony and have been in charge of the Great Basin territory. Before you joined Central you helped establish Butterfield on the Southern Overland. You're familiar with the Butterfield route between California and the Pecos River, I believe."

"That's correct," Mike said.

"You're unmarried and twenty-nine years of age. I know about your boyhood, but won't go into that. You were a soldier in the war with Mexico. You enlisted when you weren't much more than a boy. You fought at Buena Vista under Colonel Jefferson Davis."

7

"Yes," Mike said.

"You were mentioned by Colonel Davis for coolness under fire while carrying messages for him."

"Cold was the proper word," Mike said. "I was scared so stiff it took days to thaw out."

"What kind of an officer was Colonel Davis?"

"Top rate," Mike said. "The best. Very considerate of men in the ranks. A fine gentleman."

John Doe's lips pursed. "I see. You're aware, of course, that he's been elected president of this so-called Confederacy?"

"So I understand," Mike said.

"You made a great many friends in the army, no doubt, both during your service and afterward in the stagecoach business. Many of them are from the South. You were approached by a man at Fort Churchill while you were on your way here. He asked you to accept a commission as colonel in the Confederate Army. With your experience in transportation you would be a very valuable officer in any army. You refused. Why?"

Mike was frowning. "How did you know about that? It only happened two days ago."

"The Pony travels faster than the stagecoaches," John Doe said. "Why did you refuse?"

"You're at least a persistent cuss," Mike said. "In the first place this secession business is all wrong. It wasn't the first time the secess offered me a commission. This wasn't the same man, but he sang the same song. It's hotheads like him that are keeping this pot boiling. These fellows have to be squelched or they might bring on real trouble."

"You squelched him, McLish. You threw him into an icy horsetrough and told him you'd get real rough with him if you ever laid eyes on him again."

"You *have* kept close cases on me," Mike commented.

"As a matter of fact that man wasn't what he pretended to be," John Doe said. "I sent him to intercept you. Mr. Majors had received word from you that you were on your way. The offer to join the rebels was a test."

"And did I pass?" Mike asked, nettled.

"Alex had recommended you to me," John Doe said. "That in itself was sufficient. For the sake of others I had to make doubly sure."

"Recommended? For what?"

"My name," said the man, "is Roger Vickers."

8

Mike glanced at Alexander Majors, who nodded confirmation.

"I see," Mike said. He didn't see. He had never before laid eyes on Roger Vickers but the name was well known. Vickers had been connected with events in California since the days of the gold rush.

He had been instrumental in organizing the first Vigilante Committee which had brought law and order to San Francisco. Afterward, the Committee had moved to excesses, and it was Vickers who had fought it and helped bring about its dissolution. He was a leader and a planner, but he had always refused public office. He shunned the limelight.

It was understood that he was well-to-do, having made a comfortable fortune in the mines. Yet little was known about his private life. Mike began recalling other events in connection with Roger Vickers. He eyed the man with growing respect. He was remembering that Vickers had fought a duel with pistols and another with sabers with men whose political schemes he had opposed. Vickers had been wounded in both combats, but his opponents had fared much worse. One had been killed in the pistol fight and the other had barely survived the saber clash.

"What did you expect?" Vickers asked, amused by Mike's expression. "A devil with a forked tail?"

Mike shrugged. "I'm beginning to see that I wasn't brought here to while away a dull evening."

Vickers chuckled. "Alex, I believe you should first tell him what you have in mind."

Majors spoke. "We're happy you got here in a hurry, Michael. I doubted if you could make it for another day or two. That might have been too late for Roger's purpose."

"And this purpose?" Mike asked.

"If war breaks out, the Butterfield operation will be abandoned at once because it swings through southern territory," Majors said. "In that case Central Overland will finally come into its own. Central will be the only link between California and the Union. We'll be swamped with business. Enough to put us on our feet and then some." He paused and added. "Provided we can get the livestock and the coaches to handle it."

"And Butterfield has these coaches and horses," Mike said.

"Exactly. At the first sign of real trouble all Butterfield equipment as far east as the Pecos will be started on a run for California. At least as much as can be grabbed before

9

the secess do. They'll be after it, hot and heavy, of course. The Butterfield interests will operate over Central between California and Salt Lake and we'll handle it east of Salt Lake. I imagine you are beginning to see why I sent for you."

"I wish to hell I hadn't bought these new clothes," Mike said.

"Having worked for Butterfield in Arizona, you're familiar with the country and know many of their men. We want you to ride through and line up everyone we can depend on. You'll impress on station managers the importance of stocking up on fodder to care for the stock that will come through."

"Won't Butterfield send men for the same purpose?"

"Undoubtedly," Majors said. "But we don't know who they might be or on which side they stand. We do know you. We want you there on behalf of Central."

He drew a money case from his pocket. "You'll find five hundred dollars in cash for immediate expenses," he said. "Also bank drafts which will be valid only when signed by you in a sum up to five thousand dollars. That's for any unexpected expense."

"Such as buying horses?" Mike asked.

"Or men," Majors said.

Rogers Vickers spoke. "Or women?"

"Women?" Mike said. "That's the first bit of cheer I've heard."

"What we want are horses and rolling stock," Majors said. "But this is only my part of it. There's something even more important at stake that turned up after I sent for you. Roger will explain it to you."

"You talk like you're sure a shooting war is coming," Mike said.

"What else is there to think?" Majors said. "Seven states have already seceded. There'll be more. They're holding that convention in session at Montgomery, organizing their own nation and their own army. They mean business. And Lincoln has made it plain he'll send troops against them if they go through with it."

"When do you want me to start?" Mike asked.

Again it was Roger Vickers who spoke. "Tomorrow morning. A Butterfield stage is leaving at seven."

"Tomorrow morning?" Mike groaned.

Less than forty-eight hours in the past he had been helping a driver dig a stage out of mud and snow in the stormy darkness in the Carson Valley. The day before that he had been trying to sleep while lying on bulging mail sacks in a coach bouncing over a rough trail into Fort Churchill. For three days before that it had been sleet and gumbo mud across the Ute desert. He had made the last leg from Sacramento the previous night aboard a cattle boat.

In the room that had been held for him at the St. Nicholas he had found a note from Alexander Majors that directed him to their meeting place.

"I figured I'd be here for some time," he said. "I bought me some clothes. Now I'm being asked to head to hell and south into the 'Pache country."

Roger Vickers was indifferent. "You can store your foppery. Burn it for all I care. I have something more important than clothes to take up with you."

Vickers walked to the door that opened to the stairway and again spoke to whomever was above. Mike heard light steps descending. To his surprise it was a young woman who appeared.

At first glance she seemed commonplace. Like Vickers, her garb was dark and without character. She had fair hair that might have been a good tawny hue had it been given a chance, but it was combed tightly back from her forehead and drawn into a severe bun at the back. This lengthened her face, thinned it and gave the impression of hollowness of cheeks beneath high cheekbones.

Despite this, Mike saw that she was rather attractive. Quite attractive, he decided, as she moved into better light. She was slender, but appeared to be substantial enough in the correct places.

"This is Mike McLish," Vickers said. "McLish, Miss Susan Lang."

Susan Lang curtsied slightly and said, "Mr. McLish."

Her voice was carefully neutral, but she inspected him with something of the same critical disapproval he had seen in Vickers. Her eyes were a good shade of hazel and very clear.

Vickers arranged a chair for her and motioned them all to be seated again. He patted Susan Lang's shoulder affectionately. Mike frowned and gave her a second look. It was his turn to be critical and disapproving.

"Make it as brief as possible, Roger," Alexander Majors said. "I'm catching a boat for Sacramento within the hour. I'm needed back east as fast as I can make it."

CHAPTER TWO

Vickers drew his chair closer. "The other matter in which you can be of help, McLish, must be kept strictly between ourselves," he said.

"I have a hunch I'm going to hear it whether I want to or not," Mike said.

Vickers waved that aside. "There'll be a man aboard that stage tomorrow named Wheeler Fiske. Have you heard of him, McLish?"

"Vaguely," Mike said. "Politician, isn't he?"

"That's one of his qualities. He's from the southern end of the state. Los Angeles. An influential man. Wealthy. He made his money in land and shipping. He comes from a fine Georgia family. He's educated, intelligent, a brilliant orator and also a man whose word can be depended on."

"Quite a person," Mike commented.

"Yes. Wheeler Fiske is also a dedicated man and one of the most dangerous citizens of California."

"Dangerous? How's that?"

"Fiske is an ardent secessionist," Vickers said. "He first tried to maneuver California into seceding. When that failed he forced a vote in the southern counties to divide the state. The thing carried too, and by a three to one majority. Los Angeles is a hotbed of secession."

"California is going to be divided?" Mike exclaimed.

"Not yet at least. Splitting a state must be ratified in Washington. Thus far it's been blocked in a Senate committee. Fiske turned heaven and earth trying to force action. He didn't get away with it, thank God. But he's a stubborn man. He's got a far bigger iron in the fire. He's planning on seizing California for the Confederacy by force."

Mike's brows pinched together. "How, by force?"

"I happen to know that a considerable force of men is being gathered secretly near El Paso, equipped to march overland to California. Fiske is backing them and making

12

the arrangements at this end. This outfit intends to seize all Butterfield stations and equipment as they march west and then grab control of California."

Mike looked at Alexander Majors. Again Majors nodded confirmation. "Our only hope is to get our hands on Butterfield equipment before Fiske's outfit moves in, Michael," he said.

"This," Mike observed, "adds a little sticky icing to the cake."

He looked at Susan Lang. She was sitting with her hands clasped on the table. She had slim fingers with long, well-kept nails. A small, inexpensive bracelet of a type Mike had noticed in the window of a Spanish silversmith in the plaza circled her right wrist.

Susan Lang's real life, he decided, had not been spent in the drab manner her garb indicated. She saw him gazing at her hands. She gave her fingers an inspection as though making a mental note for future reference. He saw that she realized there were flaws in the role she was trying to portray.

He decided that none of what Vickers was saying was news to her. Evidently she had been called into the conference for the purpose of studying him and passing judgment on him. He resented that.

Vickers was still talking. "I am sure Fiske is also intending to bring men by sea. He chartered a schooner here, which sailed in ballast, ostensibly for the Sandwich Islands, but in reality for Panama. He—his agents rather—have bought a considerable amount of arms and ammunition in the East. We believe these were sent to some port in the South, probably in Texas. We also have reason to believe that a second force is being gathered to sail for Panama. They'll transfer, no doubt, to the schooner. Fiske aims to invade San Francisco from land and sea."

"You seem to be sure of your information," Mike said.

"I'm very sure," Vickers snapped. "I've had help from federal agencies in keeping track of Fiske's activities elsewhere. I've handled the matter myself here in San Francisco. He's been working furiously in California for months. He's had no trouble setting up his organization in the southern end of the state. But San Francisco is the key."

Mike nodded. "The money's here. The purse strings."

"Exactly. This town can be seized by surprise, particularly if there was help from within. And there'll be help, you can bank on that. San Francisco is Unionist by majority, but far from unanimously. It's full of southern sympathizers. Fiske has been here for several weeks, organizing and raising money for his coup."

"Why hasn't he been arrested?" Mike asked.

"He's just a little too powerful to handle in that way. And it might touch off the explosion we're trying to avoid. In addition, we have no actual proof. I've spent much time and money keeping tab on him. He's been seeing many people here, all of them siding with the South. Some are friends of mine. They believe they're right just as I know they are wrong. Some may be going along with Fiske, some may not. That's what I want to know. I must have names so that I can clamp down on them at the proper time. I want facts."

Majors spoke. "That's the biggest job we have for you, Michael. Bigger even than the Butterfield end of it."

"Fiske's business here is finished," Vickers said. "He's leaving tomorrow for Texas to meet Lew Durkin, no doubt, and put his scheme in operation. He has sent money back to Texas before this, but he's taking the real war chest with him this time. He's raised at least one hundred and fifty thousand dollars to the best of my information. He can hire a lot of fighting men with that kind of money, although he's already got quite a bunch assembled somewhere near El Paso."

"You mean he'll be taking that amount of money with him on the coach?" Mike asked incredulously. "Not in gold?"

"No. The majority is in government bonds which will be easy to sell in the world market. The rest is in bank notes—gold-backed bank notes. All of the bonds and bills are in big denominations. The bulk won't be much of a problem. It will be easy to carry. It probably can be carried on one's person. I'm not sure. However, the biggest part of it is in Los Angeles. Fiske probably will pick it up there on his way through. He'll leave San Francisco only with what he's raised here lately."

Mike rubbed his jaw. "Let's get around to me."

"We want you to be on that stage tomorrow," Vickers said.

"You mean you want me to steal this money from Fiske?"

"The money is important," Vickers said. "Very. Its loss probably would blow Fiske's plan sky high. Equally important are the other papers Fiske probably will be carrying. These might give us the names of the key men here in San Francisco—the ones who will help him when the time comes."

"Money or papers," Mike said. "It's stealing."

"Yes," Vickers said crisply. "Either by you or Susan. Whichever of you has the best opportunity."

Mike swung around, gazing at the girl. "You don't mean that this young lady's in on this wingding?"

"Susan will also join the stage as a passenger," Vickers said. "Fiske will be accompanied by a woman. It may be easier for a woman to deal with a woman."

"Is that what you meant when you mentioned buying women?" Mike asked.

"I doubt if this particular one can be bought," Vickers said. "Not for five thousand dollars certainly."

"This," Mike said, "doesn't seem to be in my line."

Vickers sighed tiredly. "You mean this task is contrary to your code of ethics?"

"My code has been bent in a lot of directions," Mike said. "I've busted my share of the rules, but this goes a little farther."

Susan Lang spoke. "What you mean is that you would steal an apple, Mr. McLish, or a kiss, but never a purse."

"A kiss at least, if the sign was right," Mike said. "But this is different. It seems that I'm being asked to make friends with the victims, then pick their pockets when they aren't looking."

"You are what is known as a noble gentleman," she said.

"What you're actually saying is that I'm a cautious coward," Mike said. "I won't be shamed into this by you or bulldozed into it by your elderly gentleman friend."

She sat as rigid as a gun barrel, bright color rising into her cheeks. "Elderly gentleman friend, is it?" she exclaimed. "I ought to take that fop's cane and break it over your insulting head. I'll manage without you. Gladly. I'll carry on the thieving and duplicity in my own treacherous way. Being a woman, I have none of your fine scruples, of course."

Vickers sighed again. "Let's have no more bickering. I don't give a purple hoot about anybody's scruples. This is war. I'm asking you to join in the fight, McLish. Scruples have no place in war. You know that."

"Perhaps," Mike said. "Provided this is war, which it is not. This will blow over. It always has."

"I hope you're right," Vickers said. "I believe you're wrong. The trouble is that both sides are sure their cause is just. Fiske, for instance. He's completely sincere. He thinks it'll be easy. A few shots fired and California will fall into his lap.

He doesn't think the North will fight, just as the North doesn't think the South will fight. But, in Fiske's case, I believe he's being used as a tool to start something far worse than even a civil war."

"What do you mean, Roger?" Alexander Majors asked.

"You've both heard of Lew Durkin, I imagine," Vickers said.

"Lew Durkin?" Mike questioned. "Of Durkin's Regulators?"

"That's the man. He's mixed up in this business." Vickers peered at Mike. "From your expression you seem to know the gentleman."

"Not by sight," Mike said. "I never saw him in person. Durkin and his guerrillas killed some friends of mine back in Kansas when they were raiding. But he's supposed to be dead."

"He's alive," Vickers said. "He only dropped out of sight when things got too hot for him on the border. I understand that he went to South America and carried on his trade as a guerrilla in a couple of revolutions down there. He's bobbed up again—in Texas this time."

"What's his part in all this?" Mike asked.

"He seems to be the one who's recruiting Fiske's army in Texas."

Mike frowned. Lew Durkin was the kind who turned up when better men were at each other's throats. He was the sort who looted bodies on battlefields. He had taken advantage of the bitter strife that had broken out on the Kansas-Missouri border between Free Soilers and pro-slavery men a few years earlier and had organized a band of ruffians. They posed by day as Regulators who were out to pacify the country. They rode at night wearing masks, pillaging villages and farms, robbing, burning, and raping. They had preyed on both sides with equal brutality.

"The Lord help San Francisco if Lew Durkin is ever turned loose here at the head of an army," Mike said.

Vickers nodded. "Exactly. That's why I'm wondering if Wheeler Fiske isn't being played for a sucker. Fiske is an idealist. He believes California will be glad to join the Confederacy and that even San Francisco can be converted. A man like Lew Durkin might have different ideas. This town could be looted."

"Looted!" Alexander Majors exclaimed. "That's a mild

16

word for it. There're millions here. The banks are loaded with money. Gold, silver. Why, they could——"

"Sack the town in a day, set fire to it, and sail away to South America or China or the South Seas," Vickers said. "The pillage of Rome would be piker play in comparison. And it *could* be done."

"It sounds too fantastic," Majors said.

"Maybe," Vickers admitted. "But it's kept me awake nights, worrying about it, ever since I heard that Lew Durkin was in on Fiske's scheme."

"What about Fiske's assistant?" Majors asked. "This man you pointed out to me this afternoon on the street? This Vance Calhoun?"

Vickers shrugged. "Calhoun is a puzzle. He bobbed up more than a year ago in Los Angeles. It wasn't long before he had worked his way into Fiske's confidence. It was about that time that Fiske got the idea of grabbing California for the secession."

"Do you mean you think it might have been Calhoun's idea and not Fiske's?" Mike asked.

"Fiske believes it's his."

"You think Calhoun and Lew Durkin are in cahoots?"

"I don't know," Vickers said. "That's what we must find out. That and many other things. I've tried to trace Calhoun's past, but drew only a blank. We searched his room at the St. Nicholas Hotel this afternoon. He had received a letter this morning that came by Butterfield. We thought it might have told us something. But he either has the letter with him, or, more likely, has destroyed it. Susan couldn't find a thing that was of any help to us."

Mike peered at Susan Lang. "You were the one who ransacked his room?" he questioned disbelievingly.

"That's another scruple that seems to be lacking in my makeup," she said. "I posed as a chambermaid. I had a key. It was given me by the hotel owner. He's a friend of—of Mr. Vickers. I haven't as yet got the hang of picking a lock. I'll catch on in time, no doubt."

"I'm sure you will," Mike said.

"I'm happy you think so highly of my possibilities," she replied.

Vickers raised a hand. "That will do. I want both of you to quit this barking and clawing at each other, confound it!"

Majors spoke. "So that's why you were so persistent in

keeping Fiske's carriage in sight this afternoon, Roger. You were keeping track of Calhoun."

Vickers nodded. "I wanted to make sure he didn't go back to the hotel and surprise Susan searching his room. That might have been awkward."

Susan Lang uttered a dramatic sigh. "It might also have been romantic. I must say that Vance Calhoun is a very handsome man. I saw him on the street yesterday. Tall. Perfectly groomed. Aquiline features, whatever that means. And those eyes. Just a touch of gray at the temples to show that he's lived beyond his years. He looked at me, just humble me, a girl without scruples, and my heart went pitty-pat."

"I can imagine the noise," Mike said.

"They say he has sword scars on his chest," she said. "From a duel at dawn, no doubt, over some fickle beauty who trifled with his affections. Someone like Julia Fortune, probably."

"What was that name?" Mike exclaimed. "Julia Fortune? Julia? Why, this fellow you're mooning over must be the one who landed in the mud today. Then it must have been Wheeler Fiske who horned in. He spoke to the lady, using that name. Julia."

"Lady?" Susan Lang questioned blankly.

"The dark-haired young woman who was with them. A raving beauty. Fascinating. Eyes like big pools of black ink. Red lips like——"

"Like blood," Susan Lang sniffed. "That describes Julia Fortune."

"And just who and what is Julia Fortune?"

Susan Lang shrugged. "She's the toast of San Francisco, so I'm told. She's the reigning beauty. An actress. Glamorous. She seems to do everything well. She sings. She dances. Men cluster around her like moonstruck idiots. That tells who she is, at least."

"But not what she is," Mike said. "Are you trying to paint her as a fancy woman? I can't believe that. She acted like a real lady."

"Meaning in comparison to me?"

Vickers broke in impatiently. "What's this about Calhoun landing in the mud and Fiske coming between you? Do you know these people, McLish?"

"I never saw them before this afternoon," Mike said. "It was only a minor misunderstanding."

"Tell us exactly what happened," Vickers snapped.

His tone was so demanding that Mike was again annoyed, but a look from Majors caused him to relent. He related the episode of Julia Fortune's smile.

Susan Lang's nose wrinkled scornfully. "Exactly," she sniffed. "It was just as I said. Julia Fortune flirts with every man who comes along."

"Keep quiet, Sue, while I think," Vickers barked.

To Mike's surprise, Susan Lang meekly obeyed. Vickers got to his feet, scowling at Mike and cracking his knuckles, as though he had suddenly found a very hot potato in his lap.

He finally shrugged ruefully, as though reaching a difficult decision. He abruptly offered his hand to Mike.

"Forget that you ever met me, McLish," he said. "Or that you met Susan. Forget this house. Don't come back to it. I won't be here after tonight. I rented it only for temporary use. I find it advisable to shift my base of operations often."

Mike realized that he was being dismissed. Suddenly he didn't want it that way. "Maybe I've been too hasty," he said.

Vickers shook his head. "I'm afraid any usefulness you might have had for us, even if you'd been willing to help, was destroyed by this tiff you had with Calhoun."

"But that didn't amount to anything."

"Perhaps not. On the other hand they may have got wind of why you were called to San Francisco. They may have made a guess. They could have decided to put you out of the way."

"Out of the way? You mean killed? Oh, hold on! How would they do that?"

"Calhoun may have tried to crowd you into a brawl as an excuse to kill you," Vickers said. "Or to badger you into challenging him to a duel. That would be safer for him. Don't make any mistake about him. He'll kill. He's already done so. At least two men in formal duels over women or card games. You may have been set up as an addition to his score."

"That's too far-fetched to believe," Mike said.

"Perhaps. It may have been only a casual incident, as you say. Wheeler Fiske is not the kind of a man to be a party to murder. However, the fact that Fiske interfered makes me wonder. Fiske may have agreed to having you eliminated on the basis that the cause was more important than his personal beliefs, only to have his conscience get the better of him."

"But that would mean Julia Fortune was a party to it and set the trap," Mike said. "Impossible."

Susan Lang joined the exchange. "Why impossible?"

"Well—just impossible."

"Bah!" she exclaimed. "Go back to your mountains, Mr. Michael McLish. Some designing woman will pick your bones."

"McLish is probably right," Vickers said hastily. "It was an accidental meeting, no doubt. However, we can't take a chance, no matter how remote it might be. I regret that we put him to all this trouble."

"But someone will have to go on that stage tomorrow, Roger," Alexander Majors protested. "You can't let Miss Lang try to handle this alone."

"I've got another man in mind," Vickers said. Again Mike felt that this was a difficult decision for him.

Vickers shook hands with Majors. "Alex, make sure the two of you aren't seen when you leave. Go on foot. I'll need the carriage later. Go by the back way. You'll find a lane leading to a side street. Susan will leave separately a little later. I have some correspondence to take care of before I pull out. After that I will never come back to this house."

Mike found himself being ushered out by way of the unlighted kitchen. He wanted to talk this over once more but he realized that Vickers' decision was final.

CHAPTER THREE

Mike looked back before Vickers closed the door. He saw Susan Lang still standing in the dimly lighted main room. Upon her was the same weight of responsibility he had seen in Vickers. There was now also a brooding fear. This she had kept hidden from him beneath a surface of flippancy.

Mike hesitated but Alexander Majors linked arms and said, "It's no use. It'll have to be done Roger's way. He knows. He knows much more than he had time to tell us."

Mike reluctantly let himself be led away from the shabby house. He discovered that he had forgotten his walking stick. He had left it in the house. It didn't matter. He was glad to be rid of it. Foppery, Susan Lang had called it.

They headed down a lane and emerged into a dark back street. They turned a corner into a wider street. Mike, surprised, discovered that they were not far from the plaza whose lights reflected against the fog overhead. Again he looked back. He could still see the roof of the gabled house.

Majors was walking fast. He drew out a watch, trying to make out the time in the feeble light of a street lamp. "Half an hour late already!" he exclaimed. "But I told them to hold the boat. I can't afford to miss stage connection at Sacramento."

"If you told them to hold it," Mike said, "they'll hold it." He added: "Why is Vickers taking all this on his own shoulders?"

"If Fiske is a dedicated man in the cause of the secession, then Vickers is dedicated to preserving the Union," Majors said. "In this case he's acting on the request of a man you can't turn down. Abraham Lincoln."

"Lincoln!"

"When Lincoln won in November, Vickers went back to Illinois. He and Lincoln became friends. He told Lincoln about Fiske's scheme. Lincoln can't do anything officially until he's inaugurated, but he managed to swing a little government help in Vickers' direction. But California is a long way off and federal agents have their hands full back east. Vickers has been on his own mainly. Like Fiske, he's risking a considerable fortune. He has to depend on volunteers and amateurs to help him. Persons like yourself."

"Or Susan Lang," Mike said. "She's no professional at that sort of thing. Who is she, actually? What is she?"

"I'm not sure," Majors said. "Roger didn't confide that in me. But if she's who I fear she is, then Vickers is truly——"

They had turned into the plaza and were confronted by uproar. The square was aboil. Men were milling in the street. More were pouring from the gambling houses. A bugle was blaring beyond the plaza. All attention was in that direction.

An excited youth ran past. "Hooray for Jeff Davis!" he screeched. "Hooray for the Confederate States! We'll show you blue bellies that you better mind your own business." He raced on toward the scene of the trouble.

Mike halted another excited man. This one was crimson with fury. "What's this all about?" Mike asked.

"It's them damned secess!" the man frothed. "Word just come that they've had the gall to inaugurate Jeff Davis as president of their damned rebel government."

The bugle sounded again, along with the rattle of a drum and the squealing of a fife.

" 'Dixie Land'!" Majors exclaimed. "They dare to play that here? There'll be bloodshed!"

A column of men in military formation came marching out of a dark side street, following the bugler and his drummer and fifer. Between the musicians strode a man carrying a flag. It was a banner with stars and bars, obviously hastily sewn together. Mike had never before seen that flag.

Mike recognized the bearer of the makeshift colors. He was Kirby, the stalwart firebrand who had been a ringleader during the dispute in the El Dorado earlier in the evening.

The bugle blared again, the drum rolled out a faster beat. The fife shrilled louder. These were drowned out by a mighty howl of fury as the Union adherents met the challenge by charging upon the Dixie contingent.

"You cursed, impudent rebels! Bust up the nation, would you? We'll show you!"

Yelling defiance, the Southern supporters ran to meet the onslaught, led by the banner-waving Kirby. He was hatless and his fair hair and white shirt marked him out in the mass of men.

Mike and Majors were caught between the battle lines.

22

The St. Nicholas Hotel was within reach. Mike grabbed Majors' arm and cleared a path for both of them through the turmoil. Around them the plaza was a tossing sea of yelling, fist-swinging men.

They were buffeted about but at last they burst into the haven of the hotel lobby.

"Wow!" Majors gasped.

Mike gazed out. The Southern contingent was far outnumbered but its members were battling stubbornly. However, they were being forced back. Defeat was certain.

Mike lost sight of the flag bearer. The banner was being tossed about. Both sides were fighting for its possession.

"You damned blue-nosed Yanks!"

The flag went down beneath the combatants. The hotel lobby was crowded with neck-craning spectators. Mike and Majors pushed their way to the stairs and mounted to the floor above. The hotel was fitted with a balcony at this level which overlooked the turmoil in the plaza.

A woman stood alone on the balcony. She glanced at them as they stepped from the hall door. She was the dark-eyed Julia Fortune.

Mike saw that she remembered him. His hand rose to lift his hat. He had no hat. He had lost it in the plaza. It probably was trampled into the mud along with the flag of the Dixie cause.

"Good evening," he said.

"Good evening," she replied. Her voice had depth. She had the poise of an actress. She smiled and added, "I won't embarrass you gentlemen by staying. Women aren't supposed to look at such violent spectacles."

"Let me see you safely to your room," Mike said.

"I doubt if I'm in any great danger," she said, smiling.

However, she offered no objection when he walked with her. The distance was only a few steps down the hall. She had left the door open when she had hurried to the balcony. Apparently she had occupied the quarters alone. Mike could see only feminine possessions within. It was evident that she was in the midst of packing for a journey.

"Thank you," she said dryly. "I'm sure I'm safe now."

"My name is McLish," Mike said. "Mike McLish."

"And your friend is Alexander Majors of the stagecoach firm," she said. "He is famous."

"Is that why you're letting me speak to you?" Mike asked. "Because I know Mr. Majors?"

She eyed him mockingly. "You mean because he is a rich man and that I would like to meet him because I prey on rich men?"

"And do you?"

"Do I what? Want to meet him?"

"Do you prey on rich men?"

She laughed. "Of course. Ferociously."

"Do you make any exceptions?" Mike asked. "I happen to be very unrich."

"What else have they told you about me?" she asked.

"That you are Miss Julia Fortune."

"I'm sure you learned much more than my name, Mr. McLish."

"Nothing I hadn't already learned for myself," Mike said.

"And what is that? Or am I being foolish to ask?"

"That you are a very fascinating person. Talented. You sing. You dance."

"How nice," she said. "It was a man, of course, who said that."

"Wrong. A woman."

"That *is* unusual. I'm usually torn to shreds on women's tongues."

She turned to enter the room. "Good night, Mr. McLish."

"I hope I can see you again," Mike said. "Tomorrow. A carriage ride to the beach, or——"

She had chilled in the same manner in which she had discouraged him when he had approached the carriage that afternoon. "It's impossible," she said.

"Another time," Mike insisted.

"I'm leaving San Francisco in the morning. Good night, Mr. McLish. And good-by."

The door closed. Mike returned to the balcony. Majors eyed him quizzically and he shrugged. "At least I confirmed one thing," he said. "She's leaving town tomorrow. With Fiske, no doubt, just as Vickers said."

"I'm happy that you had some reward for your effort at least," Majors said.

The brawl in the plaza still raged, but the Dixie force was in retreat, overwhelmed by numbers. Dazed combatants were sprawled in the street.

Mike glimpsed a man slipping away into hiding between buildings. He was Kirby, the fair-haired bearer of the banner. His shirt was ripped, and he was mud-stained, but seemed to have escaped major damage. Mike scowled. Kirby, it seemed,

24

was deserting the battle, leaving his followers to fare as best they could while he took to his heels.

The fighting receded away from the hotel. Mike descended to the street and searched for his hat. He found it but it had been crushed beneath the feet of the opponents.

He came upon the trampled flag of stars and bars. He rescued it from the mud and examined it. It had been cut from various materials and assembled with hand stitching.

Mike thrust the broken staff into the mud so that the flag hung free of further soiling. Majors, who had followed him, lifted his eyebrows questioningly.

Mike shrugged. "They were game enough," he said. "At least the rest of them fought it out, even if their leader turned tail and ran. This must be the flag of the Confederacy."

Majors nodded. "They adopted the design at the convention in Montgomery. Drawings came through by Pony. The newspapers printed sketches of it."

The flag had three broad bars, two of red, divided by a white bar. Its blue field carried a circle of seven white stars. These stars had been cut from cotton cloth and were not perfect in form.

Majors snapped his fingers. "Great guns! My steamboat! They'll still be waiting for me! I've got to find a carriage!"

The battle was ending, the Dixie men scattering. Mike hurried with Majors down Clay Street. They found a carriage for hire in which they clattered to the Pacific Street wharf. A packet was waiting, her safety valve popping frequently, and an angry captain pacing the deck.

Majors' luggage had been sent aboard earlier. He drew Mike aside for a final word. "All of this, of course, only shows that we can't waste any time," he said. "You've got to head for the Southwest at once."

"I'll leave on the morning Butterfield," Mike said. "I'll have to bump some other passenger to get a seat, I imagine."

"It won't be wise to ride that stage tomorrow," Majors said. "Fiske and Julia Fortune will be aboard. Roger will have whoever he's sending in your place on that stage also. You might be an embarrassment to Vickers' agents."

"That," Mike said, "was an unkind remark. So I'm just a bull in a china shop?"

Majors chuckled. "You've got plenty of work cut out for you. Bide Harris, the Butterfield manager here, has orders to give you anything you want. The same orders have been sent down the line by Butterfield to every agent. Bide Harris can furnish you with a saddlehorse, or maybe even a fast buggy, though I doubt that. Rigs are scarce. Everything is under hire. You probably can leave tonight."

"Tonight?" Mike groaned. "By saddle? For Arizona?"

"Probably by the time you reach Los Angeles Butterfield will be able to fix you up with a special coach, so that you can get a little rest on the fly. But time is precious."

Mike sighed. "And an hour or two ago I was patting myself on the back and cakewalking while I thought of what a high old time I was going to have here in San Francisco. Well, saddleback it is. As soon as I can fill my belly with some good food I'll get in touch with Harris."

They shook hands and Majors hurried up the gangplank which began to lift even before he reached the deck.

Mike returned to the St. Nicholas. The flag he had retrieved from the mud had been trampled down again. The plaza still boiled with Unionists.

Mike ascended to his room. In the mirror he morosely gazed at his fine garb. "Two hundred dollars worth of foofuraw gone to glory," he lamented. He brightened a little, struck by a new inspiration.

He adjusted his cravat, made sure no speck of dust remained on his attire, then left his room and walked down the hall to the door of Julia Fortune's quarters. Light showed at the threshold and he heard movement within. He tapped on the door.

"Who is it?" she called.

"A very rich friend," Mike said. "Mike McLish."

A moment of silence came. Evidently she finally decided in his favor, for the door opened. Mike stared. Apparently this last evening in San Francisco was to be a special occasion for her. She had changed to a dark evening gown and had arranged her hair in the Spanish style, held by a large comb over which was draped an expensive mantilla of cream-colored lace. A collar of seed pearls and earrings with pearl pendants set off the glossy darkness of her hair.

Mike made a sweeping bow. "Ah, *señorita,* I see that you are ready. Might I say that you are beautiful beyond compare? A real stunner."

She had to smile, even though he saw that she was on her dignity, and intended to put him in his place. "Thank you," she said. "What is it I'm supposed to be ready for?"

"Supper," Mike said. "You will make me the happiest man

this side of China by dining with me. We will fritter away the hours. With wine. Champagne. With song, with——"

"You *did* believe what they told you about me," she said. "Then you really are rich, and I am to prey on you?"

"About all I have is the price of a fancy supper," Mike said. "For me, that's being rich. If any preying is done, that's my privilege where beautiful females are concerned. That's a warning."

Her expression softened. He nodded. "That's better. If I offended you, I apologize. But there's no time for formality. Tomorrow you'll be gone. So I have to do something about it at once—tonight."

She was even smiling a little now, wistfully. He offered an arm. "You'll need a wrap," he said. "Not because of the weather. I just don't want other men looking at you in that gorgeous dress. That pleasure is just for me tonight."

She shook her head. "I can't join you, of course." She added, "I'm really sorry, Mr. McLish."

"Mike is the name," Mike said.

"I have another supper engagement," she said. "Good night. And again it must be good-by. And that is why I am truly sorry."

She would have closed the door but a man arrived. Again it was the one who had come between them previously. The one whose name must be Vance Calhoun, according to what Vickers and Susan Lang had said about him.

Calhoun had come from a room a few doors away. He was in shirt sleeves, and evidently had been dressing for a formal evening also.

"I'll be damned if this isn't the same fellow who was annoying you on the street today, Julia!" he exclaimed.

"You seem to make a habit of popping up at annoying times, my friend," Mike said. "You're again obscuring my view of Miss Fortune. Kindly scuttle aside."

Julia Fortune spoke hurriedly. "It's nothing, Vance. This is Michael McLish. He's a—a friend!"

"McLish?" Calhoun repeated. "Mike McLish. Oh, yes! I've heard that name. There's a Mike McLish with Central Overland. Are you that individual?"

"I am," Mike said. "And waiting for you to pop back into whatever crevice you came out of. I was asking Miss Fortune to have supper with me."

Calhoun whirled on Julia Fortune. "Surely you're not going with this fellow, Julia?"

"Of course not," she said. "I'm dining with Wheeler and yourself. Mr. McLish was only being courteous."

Calhoun surveyed Mike. "Courtesy, they say, can kill a cat," he remarked.

"The word," Mike said, "is curiosity. And it's showing all over you, like warts on a toad. If there's anything you really want to know about me, just ask."

"My interest in you is very faint," Calhoun said. "Except, of course, when you try to crowd into places you're not wanted."

This time it was Julia Fortune who moved between them. "That's enough, Vance," she said. "You'd better leave us, please."

Calhoun stood a moment, eying her as though debating whether to obey. He made his decision. He shrugged and said, "Of course, Julia."

He gave Mike a promising look and walked back to his room and closed the door.

"You must not attempt to speak to me again," Julia Fortune said.

"Because of Calhoun?" Mike demanded.

"If you mean that he has any claim on my affections, the answer is no," she said. "But he's a rather deadly proposition when he's crossed."

"I believe he thinks he has a claim," Mike said.

She did not answer that, but he saw that he had touched on a disturbing problem. "Good-by," she said with finality.

Before Mike could say another word she retreated into her room and closed the door. He stood there for a moment debating whether to insist that she answer the question that had been left open.

He finally turned away. He headed for the stairs. Calhoun's door remained closed, but Mike was certain the man was listening with an ear to the panel.

As he descended to the lobby he passed a small man who was ascending, carrying a carpetbag. The man wore commonplace garb, but was noticeable because of the lifeless hue of his skin. Even his ragged mustache and thin chin whiskers had a dusty, dry quality. It was as though some pigment had been left out of his makeup. Mike did not give the stranger a second thought as he continued on out of the hotel into the open plaza.

28

CHAPTER FOUR

Mike made his way to a restaurant named the Boston House. It was expensive and popular. Supper parties were under way in curtained alcoves. The patronage came mainly from the newly rich in the mines. Champagne was flowing.

Mike ordered supper and wine. He lingered over the meal, knowing what he was in for during the weeks of travel ahead. But there was a flaw. A gregarious man, he was keenly aware of his lack of companionship.

A waiter bearing a tray parted the drapes of one of the alcoves across the room. A diner in the booth was briefly in Mike's line of vision. It was the handsome firebrand, Kirby, who had led the Southern contingent into the battle in the plaza, then had quit the fight and scuttled to safety.

He had freshened up since that affair. He had found starched linen and wore a dark coat. He had not escaped damage entirely in the plaza. A lip was puffed, an eye was turning purple. His jaws bore cuts and bruises that had received medical attention. But, all in all, his injuries were superficial.

He seemed to have only one companion—feminine. Mike glimpsed a woman's hand lifting a champagne glass. Kirby touched his glass to the other and smiled affectionately at his guest whose face remained unseen by Mike. The drape closed.

Mike became more aware of his loneliness. He took a look at himself, thinking back over the years since he had been left homeless in an Illinois farm town at the age of twelve. His parents had been swept away by cholera, along with his only sister. An uncle who was appointed his guardian had bound him over as an apprentice to a saddlemaker at St. Joseph on the Santa Fe trail. There he had worked long hours with knife and awl and peg, receiving only coarse food and meager shelter—the customary compensation for apprentices.

It was there he had learned what slavery meant. He had been brought up to respect authority, but in this case authority was the paper that had sold him into servitude for five years.

He had endured it for a year, then had tossed his subscriber into the tanning vat and had headed down the trail in a trader's wagon as a stowaway. He had wound up in Chihuahua in old Mexico. The trader, a kindly man, had made a bullwhacker out of him.

He had stayed with the Santa Fe trail until the war with Mexico came and he had followed Jefferson Davis to Buena Vista. Returning, he had gone into stagecoaching as a silk popper, as drivers were known, first on the Missouri border and later on the big overland routes.

That was where he had picked up the piece of Cheyenne flint that still bothered him at times. It was embedded beneath his left shoulder blade. It probably would be a fairly simple matter to have it removed if he could only find the time—and the patience—to spend a few days in a bed.

Eventually he had found himself in charge of the toughest stretch of the old Leavenworth & Pikes Peak Express, as division boss. He had grown skillful in the use of his fists and also a pistol, for these formed the ruler by which a man's right to authority was measured.

After that had come Butterfield where he had drawn five hundred dollars a month because of his talent for locating and building newer and better routes through the rough stretches. He had inspirited crews into staying on the job on short rations and short water while Comanche and Apache warriors watched from the ridges—and sometimes came in to scalp.

He had always admired Alexander Majors, and that had decided him to shift to the firm of Russell, Majors & Waddell on Central Overland. Butterfield had government subsidy as well as mail contracts. It operated efficiently, but it also was under a politically inspired handicap that was anathema to Mike and every real stagecoach man.

The Southern Overland route had been chosen by the Postmaster General, Aaron Brown, who hailed from Memphis and was aware of the line's strategic value. The trail swung far south by way of El Paso and even dipped into Mexican

30

territory at one stretch near the Colorado River. The Central Overland route saved days of travel and would save thousands of dollars in operating costs. But Aaron Brown had held the whip hand.

The majority of the men who worked for Butterfield in the Southwest were personal friends of Mike. So was John Butterfield. But Alexander Majors was an inspirational leader. He was an empire builder, a dreamer who planned a network of stage lines that would help open all of the West to settlement. Majors had enlisted Bill Russell and Bill Waddell into trying to bring that dream to life.

The dream was drowning in governmental indifference. The Pony Express, which was a part of that dream, had turned out to be a nightmare financially. Now the threat of war held the promise of salvation for Central Overland.

The firebrand and his companion in the alcove had finished their suppers. The bill was paid and the waiter parted the curtains for the couple to leave. The woman wore a hat with a veil that hid her face. She had thrown around her shoulders a fur-trimmed wrap whose bulk made any estimate of her age or figure uncertain.

Mike's interest was idle. It centered mainly on Kirby because he entertained a remote contempt of the man for the way he had deserted his comrades. Suddenly his attention sharpened. The woman was drawing on gloves. She had graceful hands. Young hands. And on her right wrist a small silver bracelet that he recognized.

She was Susan Lang!

Mike half-rose, then sank back. He was sure neither she nor her escort were aware of his presence for they left the café without a glance in his direction.

Mike signaled a waiter, left a gold piece on the table, and hurried from the restaurant. He paused in the recessed doorway and peered out. Susan Lang and Kirby had walked to a carriage that stood a short distance down the curb. This vehicle, in contrast to the polished equipages that waited for other patrons, was a tough, durable spring wagon, whose purpose was service over rough trails. It had a team in harness.

Susan Lang kissed Kirby and gave him an affectionate squeeze. Then she was helped into the wagon. The team swung into the street, wheeled and passed by Mike at a stiff trot. The reins were being handled by a man who had the leathery look of a hostler.

In the band of lamplight from the restaurant window Mike saw that a carpetbag and a canvas carryall, along with hatboxes, were lashed in the rear box. Susan Lang was struggling into a dust coat. All in all, the impression was that she was setting out on a long and fast journey.

Mike stepped onto the sidewalk as though just leaving the restaurant. Kirby came walking by, passed without a glance and continued on into the plaza.

Mike debated the advisability of trailing him. He decided against it. There was something else more important.

Apparently Roger Vickers had made a mistake in trusting Susan Lang. There might be some plausible reason why the person Vickers was depending on to help block Wheeler Fiske's scheme was on kissing terms with the person who represented the fiery spirit of the southerners, but on the face of it Vickers seemed to be set up for treachery.

Vickers must be informed at once, of course. Mike was sure he could locate the shabby house again. He knew that the chances were that Vickers would no longer be there. Vickers had said he would remain at the place only a short time. However, he might have lingered. It was worth a try.

No rental carriage was in sight so Mike set out at a fast pace on foot. The distance could be no more than a dozen blocks at worst.

His course carried him through the plaza. He delayed long enough to make a hurried side trip to his room in the St. Nicholas where he opened a saddle pannier and brought out his brace of pistols.

One was a Navy cap and ball, the other a lighter weapon, intended for handier carrying. He made sure the charges and action were in order and thrust this gun in his belt.

He hurried out and headed away from the plaza. Presently he turned a corner and congratulated himself when he saw the loom of the gabled roof ahead.

His hopes fell. The house was dark. Vickers evidently had left. Mike paused on the sidewalk in indecision. He was about to turn back toward the plaza when he heard the faint thud of a horse stamping a hoof. He walked along the carriageway to the rear yard. The carriage and team that had originally brought him to the house along with Vickers and Majors stood in the stable yard, the horses drowsing where Vickers had tethered them.

Mike discovered that the kitchen door stood open. He mounted the steps and stood peering into the dark interior. No sound came. Yet, he felt that there was sound. He decided it was the throb of his own pulse.

He entered the kitchen, walking on the soles of his boots. In spite of his size he made a minimum of sound on the creaky flooring. He had learned the art of moving silently in a harsh school—on battlefields and in the Indian country.

He passed through the kitchen into the main room and groped his way until he located the table. He moved to the sideboard and his hand located the lamp. Its chimney retained considerable warmth. The lamp had not been extinguished many minutes.

He felt his way to the door which opened to the stairs. Again he listened, but the house seemed unoccupied. Susan Lang had departed also.

But if Vickers had left, why hadn't he taken the carriage?

Mike drew out his block of matches and lighted the lamp. Without replacing the shade or glass chimney he carried the light, the open wick flickering, and mounted the stairs.

There were two rooms above, opening off the small landing. Each contained a rickety bedstead, a dresser, washstand, and chair. The beds were still made up and, in contrast to the shoddy background, showed crisp new linen and new quilts.

One room retained a faint, pleasing fragrance. A fine perfume. This, obviously, was the room Susan Lang had occupied.

Mike opened the dresser drawers. They were empty. A small scrap of white cloth lay on the rag carpet, partly beneath the bed. He picked it up.

The cloth was cut roughly in the shape of a star. It apparently had been scissored from some feminine garment. Its design had not been exact and it had been discarded.

Searching on hands and knees, Mike found tiny clippings and threads in white and blue and red. Someone had done considerable sewing in this room, but had not had time to tidy up completely. The discarded white star had been overlooked.

Th makeshift banner of stars and bars that Kirby had carried in the plaza had been made in this room beyond question.

Susan Lang was not only on kissing terms with the mysterious Kirby but apparently was working wholeheartedly with him in the secessionist cause.

33

It must have been done without Vickers' knowledge. The irony of it struck Mike. In the house Vickers had used as his headquarters Susan Lang had worked diligently against him.

This made it even more imperative that Vickers be found and warned. Carrying the wavering light, Mike descended to the main room. He now discovered that one of the chairs on the opposite side of the table was overturned.

He moved around the table and stumbled over an obstacle on the floor. He recovered his balance and steadied the lamp.

He would have to search no farther for Roger Vickers. The man's blocky body was sprawled partly beneath the table. Blood matted Vickers' hair.

Mike bent over him, placing the lamp on the floor. Vickers lay twisted partly on his side. His eyes were partly open but only the whiteness of them showed.

Beside him was the walking stick Mike had forgotten when he had left this house earlier. It was broken. Nearby lay an iron poker. It must have been brought from the cookstove in the kitchen. Vickers' head bore two injuries. The assailant evidently had first used the walking stick. Probably that had only stunned Vickers. Then the poker had been wielded.

Remembering that the lamp had still been warm, Mike realized that the assassin must have been here only minutes before his arrival. Vickers still clutched a pen in his hand. Ink and a dish of blotting sand stood on the table. Vickers had been struck down as he sat writing.

Whatever papers he had been working on had been taken. His pockets had also been rifled, for some were turned inside out.

The assassin must have entered from the kitchen and crept upon his quarry. That meant that the door must have been left unlocked. Mike thought of Susan Lang. She could have left the path open for the assassin when she had left the house to keep her supper engagement with Kirby.

CHAPTER FIVE

Mike tried to assemble his thoughts and decide what next to do. Then Vickers stirred and moaned. He was not dead! Mike bent close. Vickers was breathing faintly, brokenly.

A board creaked loudly in the kitchen and Mike lifted his head, startled. Someone was there! He realized his danger, outlined as he was against the lamplight. He tried to dive aside out of the light.

That movement probably saved his life. A pistol filled the room with the glare of powder flame and with its concussion. Something grasped Mike's belt and twisted him partly around. He knocked the lamp over as he sprawled on the floor, and its glass bowl shattered.

Someone ran from the kitchen into the stable yard. All that Mike saw was the shadowy figure of a man. He came to his feet, drawing his pistol. He believed he had been hit by a bullet, but, if so, it did not seem to slow him down.

He was confused as to just where he was in the room. He collided with the table, then with the overturned chair. That cost him seconds in reaching the kitchen.

He ran into the yard but his assailant had vanished. He looked back and came to a halt. The oil from the broken lamp had burst into flame. Roger Vickers was lying almost within reach of the blaze.

Mike raced back into the house. The fire was spreading to Vickers' clothes but Mike dragged him clear, snuffed out the smoulder, and carried him out of the house.

He could not leave Vickers to pursue the assassin. It likely was useless in any event. So much time had been lost that the man was well away from the house. There was also no knowing in what direction he had gone.

The neighborhood was aroused. The fire was spreading in the house, its glare reddening the windows. Curtains began to blaze and heat cracked windowpanes.

Doors were open and voices were shouting questions. Men appeared.

Mike shouted, "Call the fire crews! Someone fetch a doctor! A man's been hurt!"

It took time to do those things. The shabby house was beyond saving before the first squad of volunteers came racing up, dragging their pumper. More crews arrived with horns blaring. They could only prevent the flames from spreading to other houses.

Mike discovered that his own injury amounted only to a bruise on his side. His belt had deflected the bullet. The slug had glanced along the leather, ripping into it, but it had saved him.

A doctor arrived. He said his name was Carver. "Why, this is Roger Vickers!" he exclaimed when he saw the patient. "I know him well. What happened?"

"Slugged," Mike said. "Footpads."

The doctor made an examination. "It might be a broken skull," he said dubiously. "A brain injury, perhaps. He's in very bad shape. I'll have to move him to my place. It looks like we'll have to operate. I'll call in some help."

An ambulance was summoned. Mike rode with it to the doctor's office. He waited in the outer room for two hours while Carver and another doctor worked on Vickers.

Vickers remained unconscious. At last the doctors came out. "It's touch and go," Carver said. "He may make it. He has a mighty tough constitution."

"Can he talk?" Mike asked.

"No. Not for hours at least. Maybe never."

"It would be better if this didn't get out immediately," Mike said. "Otherwise whoever did it might try to finish the job."

"So it wasn't footpads?" Carver said. "I didn't believe that right from the first. Was Vickers mixed up in that brawl in the plaza tonight? Is that where he got clubbed?"

Mike hesitated, debating just how much to tell. Carver shrugged and said, "I understand. There're going to be a hell of a lot more heads broken before this secession business is finished. I happen to know that Vickers is in it up to his neck. But on the right side. I'm for the Union, if that's what you're wondering about. To hell with the rebels!"

"How soon will you know what his chances are?" Mike asked.

"No telling. At least a day or two. Longer, probably. Only time will tell."

"Does he have a family?" Mike asked.

"I really don't know much about his private life," the doctor said. "I do know that he was married and that his wife died several years ago. There were children, but I'm not sure of how many or what happened to them. But he has many friends here. Someone can put you in touch with his family. I'll give you the names——"

"I'll have to leave that up to you," Mike said. "The truth is that I met Vickers only a few hours ago. In addition I have to pull out of San Francisco on the morning Butterfield. It's something I can't avoid."

He was a little surprised at hearing himself voice that decision. But he knew that he had really made that choice when the doctor had said that Vickers' chances of surviving were doubtful. If Susan Lang had any part in the attempt to kill Vickers then he meant to pin it on her.

Carver was eying him. "Just who are you?"

"Mike McLish," Mike said. "A man who tried to keep his nose out of other people's affairs and only got it twisted for his pains. If you want to get in touch with Bide Harris, the Butterfield agent here, he'll vouch for me. I'm going to be talking to Harris within the hour if I can locate him."

Carver debated it for a moment, then nodded. "All right, McLish. I guess you're mixed up in this with Vickers too. You look honest, at least."

Mike left the place and headed for the plaza. The hour was late and the sidewalks were almost deserted. Many of the gambling houses and music halls were closed, an unusual procedure, for they usually stayed open around the clock. Evidently they feared new clashes.

A lone stroller in the plaza proved to be Vance Calhoun. His straight, lithe figure was identifiable ahead as he passed across the few bands of light from windows. He was smoking a cigar and seemed at peace.

Mike crossed the plaza to avoid overtaking him. The thought was in his mind that Calhoun might have been the assassin who had escaped from the shabby house.

For safety's sake, Mike felt that he must assume that Calhoun and Fiske, or their organization, knew about his talk with Vickers and had been trailing him. That might account for the presence of Susan Lang and Kirby at the Boston

37

House. They could have been there to keep track of him.

It could have been Kirby who had followed him from the restaurant to the house and had tried to silence him. But this offered too many discrepancies. The longer he thought it over the more certain he became that this encounter with the assassin had been coincidental. Also the presence of Susan Lang at the restaurant.

He believed he had surprised the assassin who was still in the house after slugging Vickers. The man must have been hiding in the kitchen when he had entered. The assassin must have had a good look at him in the lamplight and would recognize him again even if he did not already know him by sight.

That meant that whether he liked it or not he was in this now, neck-deep. And the truth was that he was satisfied that it had turned out this way. Susan Lang's implication that he had refused to take sides because he was afraid still rankled.

There was no telling how much information they had gained from whatever papers they had seized from Vickers at the house. At any rate they had put a powerful opponent out of the way.

In the plaza someone shouted, "We'll hang Abe Lincoln to a sour-apple tree!"

That brought an outburst of profane replies and the pound of feet, a flurry of blows, and the crashing of glass in a window. That faded and the plaza became quiet again.

He located the stage office. It was dark and deserted at this hour, but he found a hostler on duty in the barn at the rear.

"Shucks, Bide Harris has been home an' sleepin' for hours," the hostler snorted. "He's married an' got a famb'ly."

It developed that the stage manager lived only a short distance away. The hostler directed Mike to the house where persistent hammering on the door finally brought Bide Harris to the door in his nightshirt with his mustache abristle.

His resentment faded when he recognized Mike. They had met in the past and were good friends.

"Sorry to roust you out at this hour, Bide," Mike said. "It's important. Company business. I want to make sure I have a seat on tomorrow's run."

"Gawdamighty, Mike!" Harris groaned. "Why don't you make up your mind? First you're goin', then you ain't. Now you are."

"What do you mean? This is the first time I've talked to you in more than a year, Bide."

"I got orders this mornin' to deadhead you through on the mornin' coach. Then, just before I knocked off for the night I get word sayin' your place would be taken by someone else. Now here you are ag'in."

"How did you get this word?"

"I got a written request."

"Who brought it?" Mike demanded.

"I don't know that I ought to say," Harris grumbled. "But I got orders to give you anything you want. The note was brought by a lady."

"A lady? Did you know her?"

"Couldn't get much of a look at her. She wore a veil and a big coat, and it was after dark. She didn't waste much time. Left in a carriage with a man."

"Veiled?" Mike exlaimed. "Of course. And the note was supposed to be from Roger Vickers."

"What do you mean, *supposed* to be?" Harris demanded, alarmed.

"What's the name of the man taking my place?" Mike asked.

"They didn't say. The note only said to hold a place open."

"Let's take a look at your passenger list, Bide," Mike said.

"Holy cats!" Harris groaned. "At this time of night?"

Harris dressed and they hurried to the station. Harris unlocked the office and got out the ledger in which was penciled the list of passengers ticketed on the morning stage.

Julia Fortune's name was there along with those of Wheeler Fiske and Vance Calhoun. Four other passengers were registered. All of these names were masculine.

"With this other man who's supposed to show up, that's all we can carry," Harris said. "We've got a load of mail to handle. It seems like a lot of people are in a lather to get back east, either north or south of the Mason-Dixon line. There's a hundred more who want fares."

Mike had expected Susan Lang to be listed. "Wasn't a Miss Lang registered for this trip?" he asked.

"Not to my knowledge," Harris said. "Who's she?"

Mike was puzzled. Roger Vickers had said positively that Susan Lang was to have been a passenger. The absence of her name might mean that there had been no need for her to make the journey now that Vickers was put out of the way.

"Hold over one of the men," Mike said. "I'll take his place. But don't bump Fiske or this Vance Calhoun."

"That's for sure," Harris said. "In California you don't push Wheeler Fiske around like he was common clay. Nor Calhoun as long as he hobnobs with Fiske."

Mike returned to his hotel. He was low in mind. In spite of the way he and Susan Lang had struck sparks she had not struck him as a person capable of treachery. On the contrary he had felt that she was too frank and outspoken for the task Vickers had given her.

When he entered the hotel Vance Calhoun was sitting in a cane chair, reading an eastern newspaper. The only other person present at this late hour was the colorless little man Mike had noticed earlier who seemed to be dozing in a chair in a corner.

Mike exercised care when he entered his room, but it was unnecessary. No assassin waited there. He slept with his pistols in reach, but he remained undisturbed.

CHAPTER SIX

It was sunup and nearing departure time when he arrived at the Butterfield station. He had stored his new garb at the hotel, hoping that some day he would retrieve it. He wore a dark sack suit, white cotton shirt, and soft-topped boots and a dark felt hat.

Wheeler Fiske was at the station, along with Julia Fortune and Vance Calhoun. The Concord was at the loading step with Bide Harris checking out baggage and mail and fending off impatient persons who were demanding fare.

Mike turned his leather pannier over to Harris, who stored it in the boot. Julia Fortune was gazing at him, surprised, and apparently somewhat disturbed. Mike guessed that she assumed that she was the attraction that had led him to take this stage. He was willing to let that belief stand. As a matter of fact she wasn't entirely wrong. But if she was flattered she didn't let him see that. And Calhoun was staring with frowning disapproval.

"Good morning, Miss Fortune," Mike said affably.

"Good morning," she said. She hesitated, then observed, "I didn't know that we were to be traveling companions."

"No," Mike said. "A happy coincidence for me at least."

Calhoun looked Mike over speculatively, but only shrugged slightly and turned away. Julia's words brought Wheeler Fiske around to gaze questioningly. Mike, in his turn, had his first real look at the man Roger Vickers held in such respect as an opponent.

Fiske was a bigger man physically than Mike had realized during that first brief encounter. He exuded vigor, but Mike saw that he seemed haggard of mouth and eyes. Here was a man whose activities were bearing heavier on him than his pride would let him admit.

Julia Fortune also seemed subdued. This morning light was quite a test of a woman's beauty, and she met the challenge. She was no girl, but a mature young woman of knowledge

41

and sophistication. She wore a dark traveling dress and carried a dust coat over her arm. Instead of a hat she wore a scarf over her hair.

Harris called for them to board the stage. Mike discovered that one of the ticket holders was the colorless little man he had noticed a couple of times at the St. Nicholas Hotel. This man was given a seat on top with the driver. Mike heard Bide Harris address him as "Mr. Murdock." Despite his appearance, Murdock evidently was a man of some influence, for it seemed that at the last moment he had displaced a passenger who was still objecting violently.

Mike studied the other passengers, trying to decide which was the one Vickers had sent to take his place.

A late arrival appeared. Mike was astounded. He was the handsome firebrand who had carried the banner of stars and bars in the plaza—the man Susan Lang had kissed when they had parted at the Boston House. Kirby! Mike carried in an inner pocket the discarded star from that banner that he had found in the shabby house.

Mike boarded the coach. He was facing Julia Fortune, who sat in the rear of the coach along with Fiske and Calhoun. Kirby moved in alongside of Mike. The third occupant of their seat was a heavily jowled man in a wrinkled suit.

Kirby spoke. "As long as we're goin' to be travelin' together, I reckon we all better get acquainted. I'm Kirby Dean."

So Kirby was his given name. "I'm Mike McLish," Mike said. "Bound east. Welcome aboard the swift wagon."

Kirby Dean was obviously startled, a fact that he tried at once to hide. He had recognized Mike's name.

Instantly it all dovetailed in Mike's mind. This was the man Roger Vickers was supposed to have called on to replace him on the coach. Susan Lang had arranged it, no doubt. Vickers apparently was surrounded by persons who were actually working for the secession. Both Susan Lang and this Kirby Dean were probably hand in glove with Fiske.

Evidently Susan Lang had told Dean about Mike's visit with Vickers. He was wondering why Mike had changed his mind and was making this journey.

Kirby Dean offered a hand. "I'm bound for Memphis. It seems like we'll be travelin' some rough roads together for the next few weeks, Mr. McLish."

He had the Deep South in his speech. Mike shook hands

briefly. He was wondering if this was the same hand that had fired the bullet that had nearly taken his life and whether it was the one that had wielded the poker on Roger Vickers.

Kirby Dean introduced himself to the others. The jowled man proved to be a cattle buyer, bound for the San Joaquin Valley. Wheeler Fiske acknowledged Dean's breezy introduction affably, but Calhoun only nodded remotely and didn't bother to shake hands.

Fiske was quietly amused by Kirby Dean's assurance. He gazed at Dean's discolored eye and other injuries. "You seem to have encountered some rough weather lately, Mr. Dean," he observed.

Kirby Dean grinned. "I run into a swing door on the outswing," he said.

"You bear your wounds lightly," Fiske said.

"You ought to see the way the door looked on the inswing," Dean said.

"Did this mishap take place last night in the plaza, by any chance?" Fiske asked. "I understand a lot of swinging was going on there."

"The plaza?" Dean said innocently. "Now, just where is that, sir?"

Fiske laughed. "You're Memphis-bound, you say? Dean? I'm acquainted in Tennessee, sir, but I've not had the good fortune to encounter any members of that family. Do you have kinfolk there?"

"No, sir. My folks are Marylanders. Baltimore. But I don't aim to go much farther than Memphis by stage."

He added with a wink. "At least not right away an' not alone. I reckon when I head farther no'th I'll have company."

Fiske laughed again. The implication was plain enough. Kirby Dean was on his way to join the Army of the Confederacy.

The stage jostled over rough cobblestones and chuckholes on the city streets. Soon it was rolling down the peninsula over a smoother clay road. Tidal flats lay on either side, gray and dreary beneath fog that was creeping in.

If Fiske was carrying the money and papers, there was no sign of their whereabouts. However, Vickers had said they would not be bulky.

Kirby Dean was talkative. He was also fascinated by Julia Fortune. He couldn't keep his eyes off her. Mike saw that she was well aware of this but she was being careful not to encourage him.

Dean spoke to Mike. "What is it I heard you call this contraption? Speed wagon?"

"Swift wagon," Mike said. "That's what the Indians sometimes call them. Mostly they call them something stronger."

"I reckon we'll be callin' this one somethin' stronger ourselves before we get to where we're goin'," Dean said. "It'll be close onto three weeks before I make it to Memphis. Somethin' tells me I'll be right fed up with these mailbags under my feet. My knees are liable to knock my teeth out any minute."

"Even mailbags get softer and softer the farther you travel, and you get so dog-tired you could sleep on a bed of nails," Wheeler Fiske said.

"I've heard tell that people's brains have been jolted out of kilter by days of this sort of thing," Kirby Dean said. "They've always been sort of touched in the head afterward."

Julia Fortune laughed. "It's hardly that bad. You'll soon begin to sink down, jolt by jolt, into a sort of apathy. You'll grow resigned."

"You'll be just like one of the mail sacks," Mike grinned.

"It's the mind's only defense," Julia Fortune said. "A form of suspended animation, I imagine. Time passes. The miles pass. Bump, crash, bang. Day and night. You finally find yourself at the destination, bruised and battered, but I doubt if your brains will be any worse off."

"Shucks, miss!" Dean lamented. "I was hopin' I could blame the condition of my brains on these swift wagons."

Mike exclaimed, "Hang on!"

Julia Fortune was already seizing a leather sling for support. Mike grabbed one also. The coach's wheels dropped into a chuckhole with a crash. It leaped upward, tossing its occupants partly out of their seats. It settled down to an even keel again, and rolled onward, its momentum unchecked.

Kirby Dean pulled himself back into his seat. He spoke wanly. "How'd you know it was comin', friends?"

"Heard the leaders jumping it," Mike explained. "Those trace chains jingle like a fire bell when the lead team vaults a chuck. You'll learn. It'll get so you'll grab for the slings in your sleep when the chains sound off."

"Sleep?" Dean moaned. "You mean anybody actually ever fell asleep on a stagecoach? Poppin' up an' down this way like fritter corn?"

44

Vance Calhoun addressed Mike. "It's rather odd that a Central Overland man should be traveling by Butterfield. Have you transferred your allegiance?"

Mike had decided from the first that Fiske and Calhoun would surmise that his trip had to do with arranging to seize Butterfield equipment in case of war. They had known that Alexander Majors had been in San Francisco, for Julia Fortune had recognized him. But whether they were aware that he also had any connection with Roger Vickers remained to be seen.

"I'm aboard on business," he said.

The cattle buyer barged into the conversation. "It looks like Butterfield's in a purty kettle of fish if this here secession business really comes to a head."

"Could be," Mike agreed.

"What's Butterfield goin' to do about it?"

Mike shrugged. "The best they can, I suppose. That's up to John Butterfield."

"They say John Butterfield's a friend of Abe Lincoln," the man said. "He won't like it if these rebels take over Butterfield, I reckon."

Wheeler Fiske leaned forward and tapped the man on the knee with a forefinger. "I don't believe the people below the Mason-Dixon line care to be referred to as rebels, my friend," he said, his jowls red. "As members of the Confederate States of America, they have a perfect right to——"

Julia Fortune's fingers closed on his arm and she was shaking her head at him entreatingly. Fiske subsided and leaned back. He produced a cigar but did not light it. He sat chewing on it. Calhoun appeared to be dozing but Mike felt that both of them were studying him, trying to size him up.

Julia Fortune sat close to Fiske and as far from Calhoun as possible. Calhoun spoke to her often, pointing out objects on the landscape, trying to make conversation. She responded only briefly. Mike decided that she was afraid of Calhoun.

Whenever she spoke to Fiske her eyes would warm and she would often give him one of her little intimate smiles. She touched his hand at times. It was an association that Mike couldn't classify. It didn't appear to be the sort of intimacy that Susan Lang had said was attributed to Julia Fortune and male companions by the gossipers. Her attitude toward Fiske was that of deep affection and respect—and also of concern.

The coach made its stations on schedule, chalking up an eight-mile-an-hour average on the good road to San Jose. Food was excellent at the noon swing stop and also the supper at San Jose. Horses and rolling stock were in top shape. Station crews were cheerful and energetic.

Mike noted these details from a professional viewpoint. Butterfield, whatever the disadvantages of the looping southern route, was operated by men who knew their business.

However, Mike learned from a station agent with whom he was acquainted, that trouble was boiling in the Apache country.

"The federal gover'ment is pullin' out all the cal'vry an' foot troops thet have been guardin' the trail through New Mexico territory," the man said. "Them 'Paches are quick to see their chance to start deviltry. From what I hear a couple o' coaches have had to make a hard run for it to get clear of some of them Injuns up in the Chiricahuas. Old Cochise is leadin' 'em."

Mike had seen the same situation developing on the Central Overland. The Sioux and Cheyennes and the Utes had been painting for war also, ready to take advantage of the chance to drive the white men out of their hunting grounds.

Darkness came. The pace slowed as the trail carried them into shaggy coastal mountains. The sidelights reflected on slants. Julia Fortune slept, leaning against Fiske. She awakened when the driver blew on his bugle. They were approaching a swing station. They all aroused, welcoming a chance to alight and stretch cramped legs.

Kirby Dean was first out of the coach when it pulled up at a rough, lantern-lit mountain station. Julia Fortune could not avoid the assistance he offered as she stepped down. He held her hand after she had alighted until she was forced to withdraw it.

"Thank you," she said. There was reproof in her voice, and also a warning.

She joined Fiske, who was preoccupied as usual with his own great plans, and strolled with him. But Calhoun stood gazing at Kirby Dean with cool appraisal.

All during the day Dean had gone out of his way to pay attention to Julia Fortune. Apparently Fiske was accustomed to this sort of thing and accepted it as the price of her attractiveness. But Calhoun was less complacent.

Mike was puzzled. He had taken it for granted that Kirby

Dean as well as Susan Lang was a member of Fiske's organization, but the growing friction between Dean and Calhoun did not fit that pattern. It didn't fit at all.

They might be only pretending, for his benefit, of course. He could not believe that. The anger in Calhoun was genuine. Calhoun, Mike conceded, was beginning to measure up to the label both Roger Vickers and Julia Fortune had given him. He seemed to be a deadly proposition.

Mike drank a mug of strong coffee in the station but passed up the flapjacks the stationmaster's wife was offering at a dollar a stack. He walked into the open and lighted a stogie.

Julia Fortune joined him. He saw that she wanted to talk to him alone. He said so that Fiske and Calhoun could hear, "They won't be harnessed for another five minutes. Time enough to do a hundred paces and back. Do you care for a walk, Miss Fortune?"

He offered his arm and they walked past the coach where the hostler and the agent were maneuvering the fresh team into position.

"What's worrying you?" Mike asked.

"Are my thoughts that easy to read?" she sighed.

"It's our friend, Kirby Dean, isn't it?"

"Yes," she admitted. "He's—he's——"

"Making a nuisance of himself?"

"Not that. But he doesn't understand. He's offending Mr. Calhoun."

"How about you?" Mike asked. "Are you offended?"

She refused that. "He's too fine a young man to—to——"

She didn't finish that either. She said hastily, "Mr. Calhoun isn't like other people. He's fought several duels. He's experienced at that sort of thing."

"I take it that you want me to call Dean aside and tell him the facts of life," Mike said. "I'm to inform him that he's blundering in where angels fear to tread and that he's likely to find himself playing a harp with these angels unless he quits trying to poach on other preserves."

Her hand fell away from his arm. "If you want to put it that way," she said rigidly. "He's romantic. It's only a passing fancy with him. He's the kind who is easily infatuated with any young female he meets."

"In this case the right word is bewitched," Mike said.

She turned to leave him. Mike halted her. "I'll speak to Dean and probably get my nose punched," he said. "I doubt if he'll listen to me in any case. However, I've got my own reasons for not wanting him killed." He added, "I was wrong. About the preserves. I'm sorry."

She did not relent or forgive him. She turned and left him. Calhoun and Fiske had stepped from the station and had been watching them. She joined them.

The coach was ready. Calhoun eyed Mike inquiringly as they took their seats, but said nothing.

Soon they were on their way again, jolt by jolt, lurch upon lurch. Mile upon mile, slow hour upon slow hour.

Mike pondered Julia Fortune's request. It might have been only another attempt to convince him there was no link between Kirby Dean and Fiske's organization. But, again, that did not ring true. She was an actress, but he felt that she had been sincere in her concern for Dean.

At the midnight swing stop he moved first and blocked Dean's attempt to alight ahead of the others. The delay forced Dean to remain seated until Fiske and Calhoun had alighted and had helped Julia Fortune down.

Dean pushed aside the elbow with which Mike had restrained him. "Now that was an unfriendly maneuver, McLish," he said.

"You're about my own age," Mike said. "Under thirty. Now wouldn't you like to live to see forty? Or even thirty?"

"I'm old enough to tell you that you're fixin' to have that arm busted right in two if it gets in my way again," Dean said.

"She's older than you," Mike said. "Maybe not in years, but in savvy. You don't know what you're getting into."

Dean twisted around and tried to launch a short uppercut at Mike's jaw. Mike had anticipated that. His fingers closed on Dean's arm, halting the blow. Dean fought to wrest away —and failed. He next attempted to brace a foot against Mike's body for leverage to break free.

Mike pinned him helpless in the seat. "Be peaceful," he said.

There was no animosity in Dean, only astonishment. "Where did you get all that muscle, McLish?" he asked grudgingly. "It doesn't show on you."

"From my dad," Mike said. "But you'll need more than muscle against Calhoun. He'd kill you in a pistol fight and think no more of it than if he'd stepped on a beetle, from the way he's described."

"And why are you frettin' about it?" Dean demanded.

"I'm wondering about that myself," Mike admitted. "Let's say that I don't like seeing blood spilled."

Dean quit struggling. Mike freed him. Dean had given no promise. Mike knew there would be none.

They alighted. The other passengers had gone into the station and had not been aware of this byplay. Only Julia Fortune suspected. She gave Mike a questioning look. He only shrugged noncommittally.

When it came time to board the coach, Dean rushed to help her, moving in ahead of Calhoun. Nothing was changed.

"You're a fool," Mike murmured to Dean as they braced themselves in their seats for the inevitable wrenching start when the fresh horses were given their heads.

"Fools sometimes win fair lady," Dean replied.

"Or a tombstone," Mike said.

CHAPTER SEVEN

They alighted in the early darkness at a settlement called Fresno. This was the second day of travel and they were already weary. They were given an hour to eat and freshen up. The unusual luxury of tubs and hot water was available.

Julia Fortune appeared in a fresh dress and joined Fiske in the eating room. Fresno was the cattle buyer's destination. A new passenger was to take the seat he had vacated.

A few minutes before departure time a dusty ranch wagon arrived with a rush. It brought a fluttery, excited young woman who possessed a carpetbag and a carryall and carried a knitting bag and reticule.

She was accompanied by a middle-aged couple. She tearfully embraced the couple and entered the coach after seeing to it that her luggage was placed in the boot. Mike and Kirby Dean, who had been standing aside, putting off the boarding of the coach until the last moment, glanced at each other and groaned.

Their new seatmate wore a crinolined dress—almost a hoop skirt. It was evident that beneath this was a goodly layer of petticoats.

All this yardage was discouraging enough, considering the confined space in a Concord. Worse yet, she wore a hat with a wide stiff brim which was adorned with streaming ribbons and an array of artificial violets and daisies. This bit of finery was fixed to her hair with two stout hatpins whose points protruded menacingly.

It was not until Mike got his head and shoulders inside the coach as he prepared to take his seat, an action that brought him almost face to face with the new passenger, that he got a look at her features in the glow of the station lanterns.

She was Susan Lang!

He should have guessed it. When he had last seen that carpetbag and carryall they had been lashed in the box of the spring wagon that had been carrying her out of San Francisco.

Recognition was mutual. Also the surprise. From her expression he was the last person she had expected to meet. She was having trouble controlling her skirts. She used that as an excuse to hide her confusion.

"Aunt Freda!" she called frantically.

The woman came hurrying. "Oh, my good land!" she exclaimed. "You'll just have to wear something else, Susan. There just ain't room for a dress like that on a stage. And you bought it 'special for this trip."

"Ma'am!" the driver wailed. "I got a schedule to keep."

"Well, you can just wait!" Aunt Freda snapped. "You'll have to get Susan's things out of the boot. The bag an' the carryall too."

The agent and the disgusted driver retrieved the baggage and Susan and her "aunt" vanished into the station.

The man who apparently was Susan's "uncle" explained the situation. "She's goin' to El Paso to marry a soldier boy. She met him last summer when his outfit was stationed near here. She's never been on a long stage trip before. She's flustered."

Presently Susan emerged, clad more practically in a simple dress and dust coat. But she still wore the flower-bed hat.

"You might as well make a clean job of it, miss," Mike said. "Throw that blasted hat into the brush. You'll do it sooner or later anyway."

"Well, I never!" she sniffed, giving him a glare. "I went to San Francisco to buy me that hat. It cost a pretty penny."

"Throw the pins away with it," Mike said. "I'd as soon ride with a bunch of porcupines."

"I just guess I won't," she said. "I might not need the hat but I'll likely need the pins against the likes of you."

She eyed Julia Fortune's more practical scarf. "Well, if it'll make you any easier to get along with," she said to Mike. She resignedly turned the hat over to Aunt Freda and fished a scarf from her bag.

"I'm Julia Fortune," Julia said, offering a hand. "And happy to have another young lady on this trip. We must stand together. However, your hat would really have been a nuisance, even though it was lovely."

"Thank you, Miss—Mrs.—For—Fortune," Susan said, stumbling over the names.

Julia Fortune laughed. "Miss Fortune. It will sound better if you just call me Julia. Miss Fortune trips a lot of tongues. And you?"

"Susan Lang."

"I understand you're on your way to El Paso to be married. How wonderful."

"I'm in such a dither," Susan said.

The driver spoke sourly. "So'm I. Let's git rollin'."

They had all alighted during the delay to put off as long as possible the confinement of the coach. Resignedly they began taking their places again. Kirby Dean offered his hand to Julia Fortune, but she did not seem to see it and stepped into the coach without help.

Mike waited until last, trying to exact the utmost enjoyment from his stogie. He tossed it away and moved to the coach to climb in.

A pistol flamed in the background. He had the impression that the bullet had missed his head only by a fraction.

He whirled, crouching. Powder smoke was puffing upward from the corner of the stage station fifty feet away. Mike had his pistol in hand. He fired swiftly, even though he had no sign of a target in the darkness. He wanted to upset the aim of the assassin if a second shot was coming.

He succeeded. The other weapon exploded again but this bullet went far wide, whipping up dust a dozen feet to his left.

Mike ran toward the station, putting all his effort into it. He heard his quarry retreating. Rounding the corner, he glimpsed a figure running in the direction of a log-built barn in the background.

Mike fired. He missed, but the shot sent the man veering to cover through the open wagon door of the barn. Mike plunged ahead, reached the barn, and crouched, restraining his breathing and listening. He chanced a glance into the dark interior. If there was an opposite wagon door it was closed, for all he saw was blank darkness. The assassin had made a mistake in trapping himself in a cul-de-sac.

Mike did not give his opponent time to settle himself. "I'm coming in!" he yelled. "Throw down your gun."

He darted into the barn and hurled himself aside, diving flat in the darkness. Three bullets came screaming around him, searching for him, but missing. He heard them smashing into the log walls close by. He kept rolling. He fired another shot into the point where the other gun was flaming.

This drew fire again. That made six bullets, Mike decided. The question was whether his opponent carried a second pistol. Mike fired again. He heard the snap of the other's weapon on an empty nipple.

Mike rushed forward, crouching, making all the noise possible, seeking to further demoralize his quarry. He wanted the man alive. This was the second attempt to kill him and there were questions that needed answering.

He had made one error. He had left the escape path too open. His quarry ran past him almost at arm's length and on through the wide door into the open.

He was outlined against the station lantern light and Mike could have shot him down with a bullet in the back. He did not want it that way. "Pull up or I'll knock your legs from under you with bullets!" he yelled.

The man quit. He halted and lifted his arms. He tried to say that he was surrendering, but was too exhausted to be coherent.

As he stood there a pistol roared from near the station. Mike heard the ball tear through the man's body. The impact hurled him off his feet and flat on his back.

When Mike reached his side the man was dying, strangling in his own blood. Vance Calhoun came walking up, a six-shooter in his hand.

"I must have notched a little too high," Calhoun said. "I only wanted to knock him down. Who is he?"

"I wouldn't know," Mike said.

The stage agent brought a lantern. "Why, this feller's one of the passengers!" he exclaimed. "He come in with you on this coach!"

Mike stared. The man whose life was draining swiftly away was the colorless one of the dusty beard whom he had noticed in the hotel in San Francisco and who had been riding with the driver during the journey. He remembered the name Bide Harris had used in addressing the man. Murdock. Mr. Murdock.

Murdock must have hung back when Mike and the others were boarding the coach and had seen his chance to fire the shot. Probably he had intended to rejoin the passengers under cover of the excitement after the murder had been committed, thereby escaping suspicion.

Murdock's halting breathing ended. His features settled into the blankness of death. Mike kept gazing, wondering if this was also the man who had tried to kill him in the shabby house.

Calhoun spoke. "He must have had a considerable grudge against you, McLish. What did you do to him?"

"Now that's a question," Mike said.

"You seem to have a talent for offending people," Calhoun said.

Mike straightened. "Now maybe you've guessed it," he said.

A bald, word-sparing sheriff named Gus Feldmire arrived shortly. He searched the pockets of the dead man, but the only identification that came to light was a tobacco pouch which bore in faded gilt letters the name "Samuel Murdock."

The sheriff was all for detaining the stage passengers, but he changed his mind when he discovered that Wheeler Fiske was involved.

"I'd appreciate it if you would call the inquest at once and take our testimony," Fiske said. "This seems to be a clear-cut case of mistaken identity. I'm very anxious to lose no time."

The inquest was held on the spot, with townspeople who had gathered serving as jurors. Calhoun testified that he had fired only to wound. Mike's testimony was brief, although Gus Feldmire questioned him closely as to any previous knowledge he had of Murdock. Feldmire, obviously, did not believe him when he insisted that the man had been a complete stranger.

The verdict was quickly returned. Vance Calhoun's action was held justified. "At least 'til somethin' else turns up," Feldmire said dubiously.

Calhoun was tight-mouthed, and there was a bleak, bitter aspect in his eyes. A sick regret. Mike believed that the killing of "Murdock" had been a calculated murder, by one that weighed on Calhoun's conscience.

Mike raked his mind, trying to recall the exact circumstances under which he had encountered Murdock in San Francisco. He recalled having passed the man on the stairs early in the evening. It was possible, he reflected, that Murdock was on his way at that moment to see Calhoun, who was still in his room, preparing for the supper with Julia Fortune and Fiske.

Later on he remembered that he had noticed the man in the lobby, apparently dozing. Calhoun had been present also.

There had been no sign of any connection between them, but Mike was convinced there had been one. "Maybe they had been waiting there for me to show up so that Calhoun could point me out to Murdock so that there'd be no mistake," Mike reflected to himself.

That would explain why Calhoun had shot Murdock down. He wanted to prevent Murdock from being taken prisoner and forced to talk.

Mike continued mulling it over as the coach rolled southward in darkness, two hours behind schedule. There was no talk. Susan Lang, whenever Mike glimpsed her face in the sidelights, was pallid and subdued. She was obviously shaken by the killing.

Wheeler Fiske also was silent and sleepless. Mike finally heard him speak to Calhoun in a low tone. "Did you know that man—Murdock, Vance?"

"No, of course not!" Calhoun snapped impatiently. "Why do you ask a question like that, Wheeler?"

"He was surrendering and had only an empty pistol, Vance," Fiske said. "You were a little hasty in shooting him down."

"I told you it was an accident," Calhoun said. "I feel very badly about it. But it's done, and can't be helped. I shouldn't have interfered in McLish's feuds. But it's over with."

Fiske dropped the subject. But Mike felt that he was dissatisfied with Calhoun's explanation.

Mike was unable to get a word alone with Susan Lang until the next morning. The stage had been ferried across Kern River, a sizable stream. He sat with her, lingering over tin cups of murky coffee in a dingy eating room after the other passengers had finished their breakfasts.

"Who were the fake relatives at Fresno?" he asked.

"They are Union supporters," she said. "Friends of Roger Vickers. That was all arranged ahead of time."

"How did you get there ahead of the stage?"

"I was driven from San Francisco in a light carriage. Fresh teams were furnished us at Butterfield stations. Now, what about you? Why are you on this stage?"

"I changed my mind," Mike said.

"Just like that. You changed your mind. Then you're beginning to believe that the secessionists are in earnest?"

"I'm here," Mike said. "That's answer enough."

"You're not wanted. You'll only be in the way."

"You mean I might upset your plans?"

"Yes," she said. "You know just enough to be a liability. One wrong word might give the whole thing away. Why did that man, Murdock, shoot at you?"

"Someone else must have decided that my presence might be a liability too," Mike said.

She studied him soberly. Her expression suddenly changed. She beamed at him, fluttering her eyelashes. "Calhoun is watching us, wondering what we have to talk about," she said. "Pretend that you're flirting with me. Act interested in me. Quit scowling at me."

Mike complied. He winked at her and laid his hand on her own. She withdrew it and giggled giddily. But she gave him a brief glare. "Don't overdo it! And don't get fresh."

"I doubt if Calhoun is interested in any carrying-on by us," Mike said. "He's busy keeping that stubborn southerner away from Julia Fortune."

She seemed puzzled. "Southerner?"

"Kirby Dean. He's making a fool of himself over her."

"He's no southerner," she said. "And I'm afraid that accent of his isn't fooling anyone. Su᷄ ᷄ you know that he's the one who took your place on the stage after Roger Vickers decided it wasn't best to send you?"

"I see," Mike said.

Again he was at a loss as to whether she was on the level, or whether she surmised that he was aware that she had arranged Kirby Dean's fare and was going along with that obvious explanation. But she had much more explaining to do. The cloth star that he had found in the shabby house, for one. And Kirby Dean's leadership of the secessionists in the plaza when he had carried the flag she had made.

"Do you mean Mr. Dean's in some kind of trouble?" she asked.

"He's probably digging his own grave," Mike said. "I think he's going to find himself called out one of these days."

"Called out?"

"To a duel. That's said to be Calhoun's speciality."

"Oh, my goodness!" She seemed appalled. She gazed through the dust-fogged window at Kirby Dean who stood outside moodily watching Fiske stroll with Julia Fortune. She was deeply worried. And perhaps jealous, Mike reflected, remembering the tenderness with which she had kissed Dean good-by in San Francisco.

She pushed aside her coffee. Her gaze rested on Julia Fortune. Mike saw her lips tighten.

"In all fairness, Julia Fortune isn't to be blamed," he said. "She's done her best to discourage him."

"I'll just bet," Susan said grimly.

"What's she supposed to do?" Mike asked. "Kick him on the shins to let him know he's out of line?"

"Dean was always a fool when it comes to women," she said. "I'll give him a talking to at first chance."

"You know him well, then?" Mike asked innocently.

"Yes," she said grimly. "Very well."

"I noticed that it was his shoulder you slept on in the coach last night," Mike said.

She looked down her nose at him. "Apparently yours was available."

"What I mean is that you're supposed to be engaged to some mythical person in El Paso," Mike said. "Aren't you inviting suspicion by showing interest in another man?"

"Men," she corrected him. "They've seen me flirting with you. I've even fluttered my eyes at Calhoun. I want them to label me as just a feather-headed, man-chasing female."

"Why a soldier at El Paso?" Mike asked. "Is he supposed to be a secess? Are you posing as a Unionist or a rebel?"

"That," she said, "is for them to decide. I want them to think I'm too flighty to know what such a thing is all about."

Mike was blocked again. If she had any connection with Fiske she was very adroit at avoiding any slip of the tongue that would betray her.

She was watching him. "You have your doubts about me, haven't you?" she demanded.

"Now why would I doubt you?"

She did not pursue the subject. "As long as you've counted yourself in on this after you said you wouldn't, you might as well give us what help you can. Have you learned anything?"

"About what?"

"About the money, of course, and the papers we want to get our hands on."

Suddenly Mike believed he had the answer. The money! That was what Susan Lang and Kirby Dean were after. A hundred and fifty thousand dollars was the stake Roger Vickers had said that Wheeler Fiske would be taking with him to Texas.

57

"I haven't tried," Mike said. "It might spoil things. It's too early. Vickers said Fiske would pick up the bulk of the money in Los Angeles."

"You're right," she said. "We'll hold off awhile. What do you think of Julia Fortune?"

"Interesting person," Mike said.

"One smile from her and you'd probably sell your soul."

"What's the going price for souls today?" Mike inquired.

"Maybe you can tell me," she said.

The driver sounded his bugle. "Pile on the chariot, folks," he shouted. "Next meal stop, Fort Tejon. They feed good beefsteak there an' you kin buy whisky."

Julia Fortune waited for Susan to join her before boarding the coach. "If Mr. McLish will trade places with me for a while we can chat and get better acquainted," she said.

Mike sat alongside Wheeler Fiske in the rear seat. Julia Fortune was careful to take the outside seat on the forward cushion so that Susan was between her and Kirby Dean.

Mike surmised that Fiske had asked Julia Fortune to try to learn more about this Susan Lang. Susan was still attempting to pose as a fluttery, starry-eyed bride-to-be, but she had made a mistake in adopting that role. She was unable to fit convincingly into such a picture. In spite of herself it was evident that she had education and training in the social graces.

Fiske and Calhoun were wondering about her, no doubt. If she was really here on Roger Vickers' behalf she might be in a dangerous position. The killing of Murdock at Fresno had brought to light the really ugly side of all this move and countermove jigsaw.

On the other hand all this posing might be aimed at him to lull him into believing that she was still carrying out Vickers' orders when the truth was that she was working for Fiske.

Fiske engaged Mike in conversation. "First," he said, "we will damn the weather and the discomforts of stage travel. That's the customary opening gambit in becoming acquainted."

Mike grinned. "With that out of the way, what do we take up next—women or taxes?"

"The ladies, by all means," Fiske chuckled. "That is a much more entertaining subject."

Fiske proved to be an informed and interesting conversationalist. He too had fought in Mexico. He and Mike found common ground on that subject.

"You support the northern states, I take it, McLish," Fiske finally said mildly.

"Yes," Mike said flatly.

Vance Calhoun, who had taken no part in the conversation, spoke now. "You're on the wrong side, McLish."

"I'm sure that I'm not," Mike said.

Calhoun started to press the issue but Fiske said, "This is hardly the time or place to debate it. Let's stay on neutral ground as long as we're crowded together in this infernal thing."

But the issue was clear-cut.

After that they were silent, watching the empty land flow by. Dreary flats of sage and rabbit brush stretched on either side of the trail. The sun faded into a gray overcast. The wind developed a keen edge. At the next swing station the storm curtains were buckled in place.

Rain began, the dreary California rain of February. The driver halted long enough to don a slicker. The two passengers who had been riding on top descended and crowded into the interior, the jump seat being sprung into place.

The eight humans, with knees at uncomfortable angles, huddled wretchedly in the jolting vehicle. Rain sprayed around the curtains. They struggled to protect themselves with slickers.

"Stuff and feathers and abomination!" Susan Lang said.

"My sentiments exactly," Julia Fortune sighed.

CHAPTER EIGHT

They pulled into the flat-roofed, mud-swamped town of Los Angeles late in the afternoon the next day. The rain still beat down and was whipped against the adobe walls by a bleak wind.

"Four hours' rest," the driver said. "You'll have a new silk popper on the box from here to Termescal. *Adios!* Watch out for thieves, bad women an' three-card monte sharks. This hellhole is full of rascals."

Again Mike saw the flag of stars and bars. One hung in the rain from a staff above a building across the street. Others were displayed in shop windows. These were makeshift flags, like the one Susan Lang had sewn in San Francisco. In spite of the rain a straggling parade marched by, following a line of drummers, and they too carried the flag of the Confederacy.

Los Angeles, it seemed, was ruled by the secessionists.

They trooped into the little lobby of the Bella Union Hotel. Kirby Dean was at Julia Fortune's side. "I'd consider it a mighty big honor if you'd join me at supper, Miss Fortune," he said.

Calhoun roughly pushed Dean back. "Stay away from Miss Fortune," he said.

Dean's recovery was swift. He lashed out with a fist that Calhoun only partly avoided. Its force sent Calhoun reeling and left a white, bloodless blotch on his cheek.

Calhoun's hand sped inside his coat and came out with a pistol. He would have shot down Kirby Dean but Mike caught his arm, so that he could not point the weapon.

"Stop it!" Mike snapped. "This is no place for a shooting!"

Calhoun controlled his anger. "I'll be at your service, fellow," he said to Dean. He had become stiffly formal. "Or do you know what that means?"

"I know," Kirby Dean said. "Name the time and the place."

"No!" Julia Fortune cried frantically. "No! There's no cause for a duel. Stop it! Stop it, Vance!"

Dean spoke to Mike. He was pale. "Will you act for me? I believe it's my choice of weapons. I'll take pistols."

Mike was angry but helpless. Didn't Kirby Dean realize that he was in too deep? "I want no part of this," he said. "Calhoun, you're making too much out of this. Both of you were wrong. Cool down now."

Fiske, who had been at the desk arranging accommodations, came hurrying. "This is impossible, gentlemen," he said. "Vance, you must withdraw your challenge. As for you, Dean, I must insist that you pay less attention to my fiancée's welfare. I'm capable of looking out for her comfort. If a duel becomes necessary it will be my privilege, not Mr. Calhoun's."

Kirby Dean was gazing, appalled. "Your fiancée?" he mumbled.

"I have that happiness," Fiske said.

Calhoun also seemed thunderstruck. He whirled on Julia. "Is that true?" he exploded.

"Why not?" she replied. She walked to Fiske and kissed him on the cheek.

Kirby Dean was ashen. "I congratulate you, sir," he said to Fiske. "My best wishes for your happiness, Miss Fortune."

He looked at Calhoun. "I decline your challenge," he said. "I was in the wrong." He walked out of the hotel.

Even Calhoun seemed embarrassed. He laughed uncertainly. "I've never seen a man turn as yellow," he said. "It makes a person feel squirmy."

But Mike had seen the urgent message Susan Lang had given Dean with her eyes. It had not been cowardice or even chivalry toward Julia Fortune that had caused Dean to show the white feather. He had received an order that there was bigger fish to fry than for him to risk a duel.

Mike moved to the desk and rented a room, ordering a tub and hot water. As he mounted the stairs Susan joined him on her way to her own quarters. A porter followed, carrying their luggage.

"You were right," she murmured. "My respect for Julia Fortune continues to grow. She's not what some people say."

"You think she's not as scarlet as she's been painted?"

"As I painted her. That's what you mean, isn't it?"

"Did you decide this because Wheeler Fiske is going to make an honest woman of her?" Mike asked.

"Bosh! She's no more engaged to marry Fiske than she was before. Which was never. Fiske only said that in order

61

to avoid that foolish duel. He probably needs Calhoun's help in more important matters and couldn't take a chance on him being killed."

"You might be right," Mike said.

"Fiske placed her in an awkward position. She couldn't make an idiot of him by denying it in front of everyone. Then nothing would have stopped the duel."

"Calhoun probably would have killed our friend Dean," Mike said. "You know that, don't you?"

"Yes. I'll be eternally grateful to Julia Fortune."

She entered a room and the porter led Mike on to his own quarters. As he shaved and splashed he kept thinking over what Susan Lang had said. She was grateful to Julia Fortune for making a small sacrifice that might have saved Kirby Dean's life. And yet Dean was neglecting her while he pursued the other woman.

"It must be true love," Mike reflected tiredly. "I'll never savvy these females."

But it still didn't add up. Susan Lang didn't size up as the kind to let a man be taken away from her without considerable fur flying.

"She ought to be in a mood to claw Julia Fortune's eyes out," Mike ruminated, consulting his freshly shaven features in the mirror. "But all she does is act sweet and thankful."

He changed to fresh linen. In the pocket of his coat he came upon the white cloth star. It was already becoming pocket-worn. He gazed at it and all the suspicions of Susan Lang came back. He pocketed the star again and went down to the dining room.

He ate among strangers at a long table where the dishes were passed from hand to hand. A waiter told him that Susan Lang and Julia Fortune were being served in Julia's room.

From the window of his room he had seen Fiske leave the Bella Union in a carriage shortly after their arrival. He had not returned. Calhoun and Kirby Dean also seemed to be dining elsewhere.

Rainy darkness had come when the passengers began assembling in the hotel office to resume the journey. Calhoun came walking in from the street wearing a dripping slicker. Fiske returned in a carriage. He bore the look of a man who had completed a busy and satisfactory day. Furthermore he carried under his arm a leather dispatch case which seemed to be comfortably filled.

Mike felt a humming surge of elation. Susan Lang gave him a sidewise glance. She was excited also. They both were sure they knew what that satchel contained.

Afraid that he might betray his thoughts, Mike walked to the clerk's desk and bought an additional supply of stogies. He also bought a copy from a stack of newspapers that had just been brought in. Los Angeles supported a publication called the *Star* Advertisements for patent medicines occupied a major portion of the front page.

One column bore in large type the word: "Important!"

Susan Lang was attracted by this large type and came to stand at his elbow to read also. He glanced through the subheading and looked up at her, startled.

It was an account of the attempt to kill Roger Vickers, which was fresh news for the semiweekly Los Angeles paper.

Susan Lang uttered a sighing half-scream. She looked numbly at him and tried to grasp the desk for support. He moved in time and caught her before she fell.

"A lady's fainted!" a bystander babbled. "Fetch the smellin' salts!"

Julia Fortune took charge. "Carry her upstairs, Mr. Mc-Lish," she said. She led the way to the room Susan had occupied.

Mike placed the limp girl on the bed and stepped out into the hall while Julia Fortune and a Mexican woman housekeeper applied cold cloths and loosened stays on the patient.

Mike still had the copy of the newspaper, somewhat crumpled, and he hurriedly read the article. The account of Roger Vickers' injury had come by telegraph over the newly opened line between San Francisco and Los Angeles and carried late details.

Julia Fortune called, "She's all right now, Mr. McLish. You can come in if you wish."

Susan Lang had revived. She looked up at him and at the newspaper in his hand. Memory came back. He saw horror rise in her eyes. And grief.

Julia Fortune was busy preparing a new damp cloth at the washstand across the room. Mike bent closer over Susan. "Vickers is alive," he murmured. "You didn't read far enough. He wasn't killed. The doctors say he'll pull through."

She began to sob. Deep, heartfelt sobs. Julia came hurrying and soothed her. "It must be the excitement of the trip, you poor dear," she said. "You'll have to rest here for a day or two. You can catch another stage."

Susan mastered her emotions. "Oh, no," she exclaimed. "I'm all right now. I can't wait. Tom—Tom was to get leave to meet me in El Paso. I just can't take a chance on missing him. I might not be able to get a seat on another stage for days, they're so crowded."

"Tom" was her mythical fiancé.

"Are you sure you're up to it?" Julia asked.

Susan sat up and got shakily to her feet. "I'm sure," she said. "I'm all over it." But she was still shaky and without color.

Mike was again at sea. She had taken it for granted that Vickers was dead when she had read the first few words of the headlines. Probably what had felled her was the realization that she was a party to murder.

But the grief? That had appeared genuine. Mike's name had not appeared in the news story. It said that a passer-by had carried Vickers from the burning house. Susan had no way of knowing that he had previous knowledge of the attempt on Vickers' life.

She insisted that she was able to return to the lobby. Mike walked with her down the stairs and she clung tightly to his arm.

The stage was waiting at the curb. The rain beat down on it and dripped from the dejected horses. The new driver was wrapped in oilskins and was impatient to get his dreary task started.

Kirby Dean arrived out of the darkness. He was rain-soaked, for he had not worn a slicker. Evidently he had spent his time at a cantina, drinking. He was unsteady on his feet, but he took his place in the coach without apology or humbleness.

The coach lurched away through the muddy streets. The rain never ceased. Two prospectors, bound for Fort Yuma, had replaced the men who had traveled with them from Fresno. The close-packed passengers clung to the slings and to each other in chill discomfort.

Mike discovered that Susan Lang was sobbing silently at his side. He realized that she was weeping for Kirby Dean and his shattered pride at backing out of the duel with Calhoun. Dean, despite his drinking, sat rigidly aloof and awake alongside her. If he was aware of her grief and its cause, he gave no sign. He rode alone with his own knowledge of disgrace.

Mike remained awake. He waited until all of the others seemed asleep. The leather dispatch case stood wedged between Fiske and Julia Fortune as they slept.

He leaned forward, a fraction of an inch at a time, so as not to disturb his seatmates. By stretching he might be able to reach the case and slowly draw it clear.

After that he had no plan. It was vaguely in his mind that he would leave the coach and make his way back to Los Angeles on foot with the case. Vickers evidently was out of danger and could give him instructions by telegraph from San Francisco.

The sidelights, dim in the rain, showed the dozing passengers in grotesque poses as the coach jostled them around —likes corpses in a carousel. Julia Fortune moved in her sleep, changing position slightly.

The flickering light revealed something new. The handle of the dispatch case was circled by a steel chain. It was light but strong. The other end of the chain was clamped around Wheeler Fiske's wrist and held by a small padlock.

Mike sank back. He was defeated, at least for the moment. He realized that Susan was awake and had been watching. He glanced at her. She had seen the obstacle also.

"Damnation!" she murmured dismally.

"You can double that and paint it red," Mike growled. Presently he also slept.

The trail carried them into the Laguna Mountains the next day. The rain ended, but the clouds hung low as the coach swung over endless curves in a rough trail through tangled mountains. The wet chaparral was as thick as the fur on an animal's back.

It was late in the afternoon when Mike pointed. "There it is!"

Everyone gazed. "What is it?" Calhoun asked.

It was Julia Fortune who answered. "The desert."

Calhoun sank back. "Is that all?"

"That's the start of it," Mike said. "We'll be with it for well on a thousand miles."

"It will be with us, rather," Julia Fortune said.

"You've traveled this stretch by stage?" Mike asked.

"A round trip," she said. "Two years ago. I came west in summer."

"That's one blessing we have," Mike said. "We're early

65

enough in season so that we'll miss the real heat, though we'll likely get a taste of it later on. But there'll be dust and sand and alkali."

He was about to add, "And maybe Apaches." But he didn't say it. They would learn that soon enough.

They were entering that stretch of the Butterfield with which he was very familiar. He was meeting men at almost every station whom he had known when he was working for John Butterfield. From them he had learned that the Indian trouble ahead was growing in violence.

The station agent at Warner's Ranch had bleak information. "A westbound stage was jumped by Cochise's bunch in Apache Pass a few days ago. Lost the driver, but the rest of them got through after a fight. Them Chiricahuas jumped a swing station the next day, run off the stock an' scalped a hay hand."

The coach emerged from the mountains and at sundown arrived at Vallecito on a flat overlooking the desert. No fresh stock was available. The horses in the corral had seen recent hard use.

"Them animals will be in shape by mornin'," said Amos Decker, the station manager. "Better to lay over here tonight, folks, than start out in the dark with jaded stock. Stages from the east ain't comin' through, regular. Fact is none has come through a'tall for a couple o' days."

Decker turned over to Susan and Julia his own quarters in the station.

"The men kin bed down in the main room," he said. "Or in the haystack if they want. You people are lucky. It's a lot more homey here than at Yuma or Tucson. Them places air full o' fleas, scorpions, Pima Injuns an' hoss thieves."

Mike found a chance to speak to Fiske alone. They walked in the twilight, smoking. The skies had cleared. Sunset lingered over the mountains. The first flowers of the season brightened the desert. The flats, which Mike remembered as dreary wastelands in the summers he had spent there, were now decked out in gold and royal blue and ruby red. Even the cactus bore blossoms of unbelievable delicacy.

Honey mesquite trees flanked the station which was made of adobe and more commodious than most. A spring fed a marsh.

"It might be well if Miss Fortune took the first stage back to San Francisco," Mike said.

He expected to be told to mind his own affairs but Fiske

only shrugged and said, "I've already so advised her. I did not want her to make this trip in the first place."

He paused and added, "It was a waste of words. It seems that she's very fond of me. More so than I deserve. She feels that she must look after me."

Fiske was carrying the dispatch case, which he never let out of his sight. He shifted it to his other arm. He seemed to be about to divulge some confidence, then thought better of it. "I doubt if I could prevail on her to turn back," he said.

"There can't be much danger as far as Tucson," Mike said. "If the Apaches haven't simmered down by that time, maybe she can be talked into it. And Miss Lang too."

"Perhaps," Fiske said dubiously. "Why are you going ahead in the face of such difficulties, McLish? This stagecoach business must be very important."

"It is," Mike said.

"And this business, no doubt, is mixed up in problems in which both of us are interested?"

Mike saw that Fiske was trying to force an issue in a search for information. He met it for it might give him a hint as to whether Fiske suspected that he was involved in Roger Vickers' plans also.

"If you mean that I'm interested in taking over Butterfield equipment for the use of Central Overland," he said. "The answer is yes. I'm sure you had guessed that."

Fiske smiled. "You're frank at least. Yes, I knew that probably was the reason. Everyone knows on which side I stand. You're not in agreement with me. I regret that. I would prefer to have you with me, not against me."

"Is it necessary to be either for you or against you?" Mike asked.

Fiske's eyes became bleak and uncompromising. "Under the circumstances, yes."

"Then I'm against you," Mike said.

On that note they parted. Fiske walked to join Julia Fortune. Calhoun was with her, but she left him and came hurrying to meet Fiske and take his arm. Calhoun watched this, his eyes showing nothing, then turned away. But Mike, more than ever, felt there was both despair and a seething resentment in the man.

Mike pondered his talk with Fiske. He had imparted nothing that Fiske didn't already know. On the other hand he had gained something from Fiske. The seizure of Butterfield was a part of Fiske's plan also, beyond a doubt. The line would be valuable to any force trying to march overland to California.

Mike talked privately with Amos Decker. The agent was a veteran of stagecoaching. He and Mike had worked together when Butterfield was being placed in operation.

"Stock up on any hay and grain you can lay hands on," Mike said. "There's likely to be a lot of livestock come trailing through here one of these days."

"I ketch on," Decker said. "But where'n blazes do I dig up any fodder at this tag end of winter? I purely don't know."

"Do what you can," Mike said. "I saw that some of the ranchos this side of San Felipe still had hay in ricks. They might sell some. Sam Ross, at Warner's, might be able to scare up more than he needs. At any rate stock shouldn't arrive here in bad shape. There'll be graze on the desert, provided this thing comes off early enough. If it hangs around until summer I wouldn't give much for the chances of getting any horses through."

"It'll warm up soon," Decker said. "You'll see. It's mild now, but summer hits early in this damned country. But there might not be much stock to shove through, early or late."

"You mean the Apaches?"

"I don't mean nothin' else. Things are in bad shape east o' Tucson. Worse'n I wanted the ladies to find out."

"They might clear up before we get that far," Mike said. "One thing more about this fodder if you stock up on it. If the wrong people show up, burn it."

Amos Decker grinned bleakly and nodded. "An' run like a whitehead so they won't ketch me an' string me up fer it," he said.

Susan found a chance to speak to Mike alone. "This might be our best chance to get that dispatch case," she whispered. "At least Fiske and Julia will be separated. We must try it tonight. The farther they travel east the poorer our chances are."

"What've you got in mind?" Mike asked.

"It's that confounded chain," she said mournfully. "I've tried to find something that would cut it, but with no luck."

"You mean something like this?" Mike asked. He gave her a glimpse of a short-handled pair of metal snips, of the kind used by blacksmiths, that he was carrying in a pocket. "I picked these up at Warner's Ranch."

She was elated. "Just the thing. I wonder if Fiske will keep the case with him. Julia sometimes carries it locked to her wrist."

"Meaning that if Fiske keeps it you want me to try to relieve him of it?"

She eyed him. "I did have such a thought in mind."

"Let's start being at least partly honest with each other," Mike said. "If Kirby Dean is the one Vickers sent in my place, why don't you ask him to perform this bit of thievery?"

"I've done just that," she said. "He will try it if the chance comes, just as I hope you will also if you have the opportunity."

"I have a hunch I'll be the one who'll get the first chance," Mike said.

"Now, exactly what do you mean by that remark?"

"What if it turns out that the case contains only personal valuables?" Mike asked.

"I doubt that. But I still don't follow you."

"If Fiske or Calhoun shot down a thief they caught robbing them it would be a justifiable killing in the eyes of the law, if the law ever became interested in what happened out here. Calhoun has already gotten away with one killing. This time I'd be the one who was punctured. Your precious Kirby Dean would still be safe and alive."

She had been standing straighter and straighter, her eyes growing more and more angry. "That's an awful thing to say," she said. "It's an awful thing to think about me."

"But I could be right," Mike said.

"You think I might be working with them?"

"No," Mike said. "I did at first but not now. This is for yourself. And your friend Dean."

"For myself? Now why would——?"

"For one hundred and fifty thousand dollars," Mike said.

She was furious. He believed she would have slapped him, but at that moment Julia called to her. "I'm turning in, Susan. Come whenever you're ready."

Julia was carrying the leather case. It was padlocked to her wrist.

Susan gave Mike a withering look. "Give me that thing," she said.

She took the metal snips almost forcibly from his hand

and dropped them in her reticule. "You're safe enough now," she said.

She joined Julia and they entered the agent's small quarters in the station.

CHAPTER NINE

The men were bedded down in the larger room. Fiske slept on the only cot available. Mike and the others, including the two prospectors, stretched out on the floor on straw pallets that Amos Decker provided. "With the compliments of John Butterfield," Decker had said.

Mike awakened when any of the others stirred and sometimes even when mice and pack rats scuttled in the thatched roof. He envied Amos Decker and his hostler, who had preferred the comfort of the haystack near the corral. Mike would have preferred that sort of bed also except that he wanted to be on hand if any activity took place at the station.

After some two hours, Kirby Dean carried his pallet and blanket outside, muttering that he preferred the open air. He made his new bed in the shadow of the portico which flanked the structure.

The door of the main room had been left open for air. Mike shifted his own bed slightly so that he had Dean's new position in sight. The room where the young women slept also opened onto the portico. Mike suspected that Dean had chosen his sleeping place so that he would be handy in case Susan Lang wanted to get in touch with him.

But an hour dragged by and Dean seemed sound asleep. Mike aroused suddenly, realizing that he also had dropped off, and perhaps for some time.

Through the open door he could see the stars blazing in a velvet desert sky. Susan Lang in night clothes was crouching beside Kirby Dean, who was sitting up. She was handing him a square object. Fiske's dispatch case!

She retreated silently into the agent's room. Mike became aware that Fiske's breathing had changed. Fiske was awake. He must have seen that stealthy exchange. In the next moment Mike realized that Vance Calhoun was awake also and had been watching.

Kirby Dean pulled on his boots and tiptoed away from the station, vanishing in the direction of the mesquite trees near the swamp. Neither Fiske nor Calhoun made any attempt to stop him.

Mike pretended to be asleep. He was baffled. This was a trap of some sort. But for whom?

He heard Fiske murmur something to Calhoun. He could only make out the words " . . . at least now we know. . . ."

Presently he was sure Fiske was sleeping. Genuinely asleep. Calhoun was breathing deeply also, but Mike knew that he was only pretending slumber. Calhoun was awake—waiting.

Kirby Dean was gone so long Mike began to doubt that he would ever return. Then he reappeared out of the starlight and moved stealthily toward his pallet. He no longer had the satchel.

Calhoun sat up. He was lifting a pistol. He meant to shoot Dean down just as he had slain in cold blood the man, Murdock, at Fresno.

The open door, which was made of heavy planks slung on iron hinges, was within reach of Mike's legs. He drove a foot against the portal, slamming it shut.

Calhoun could not stay his shot. The pistol exploded and the bullet smashed into the planks of the door. The concussion filled the dark room with powder fumes and dust.

Fiske spoke hoarsely. "Good God, Vance! You didn't kill that boy? You didn't, did you? There was no need!"

"Hold your tongue!" Calhoun snapped.

Calhoun tried to open the door, but Mike came to his feet and deliberately blundered into him in the darkness, fending him off, for he knew that if Kirby Dean was still in sight that Calhoun would shoot him down.

Calhoun jammed a shoulder against Mike, unbalancing him and pushing him aside. Calhoun managed to get the door open.

But Kirby Dean was not visible in the starlight. His voice spoke from a corner of the station where he had taken refuge. "What's wrong? Who fired that shot?"

Calhoun walked into the open and Mike followed him. The waxing moon had set back of the mountain rim and there was only the blackness and the stars. Susan and Julia Fortune, wrapped in quilts, were peering from the door of their quarters, calling excited questions.

Calhoun stood glaring around, trying to locate Dean's position. Fiske shouldered past Mike, grasped Calhoun's arm and pushed the gun down. "Stop it, Vance!" he commanded.

Calhoun spoke. "I spotted a thief sneaking away from the room the women are in. He's probably robbed them."

He looked at Mike. "You're handy with your feet, McLish."

"It could have been the wind that blew the door shut," Mike said.

"And you could have been in on it with this thief," Calhoun said.

"A statement like that needs a little backing up," Mike said.

"Yes," Calhoun said. "I'll be happy to do the backing."

Mike set himself for battle, but Fiske pushed between then. "Hold on, Vance!" he commanded. "This is the second time I've had to keep you two apart. Again I insist that this is no time for brawling. Everybody's excited. What I want is to get to the bottom of this affair."

He called to Julia. "Was anything stolen, dear?"

"Yes," she answered. "Your dispatch case. It's gone!"

"What?" Fiske exclaimed. "Good God!"

But Mike decided that he wasn't as appalled as he pretended.

"The chain was cut somehow," Julia said.

Amos Decker and his hostler arrived from the haystack, stuffing shirts into pants. "Fetch a light!" Fiske commanded. "We've been robbed."

Kirby Dean, deciding that it was safe, came from his refuge around the corner of the station and joined them.

Decker ignited lanterns. By that light Julia displayed the severed chain. Fiske found the metal snips lying on the floor of the room.

"What was in the case?" Mike asked.

"Valuables!" Fiske snapped.

"Do you mean money, sir?" Kirby Dean asked innocently.

"Yes. A considerable sum. And personal papers that were worth even more to me."

"What did the fellow look like?" Dean asked Calhoun.

"You should be able to answer that better than me," Calhoun said. "You must have got a look at him."

"I'm such a danged sound sleeper it always takes me a little time to get the wool out of my eyes," Dean said. "By that time it was all over. Now, that's a downright shame. Me layin' there asleep while a cussed thief sneaks in an' robs a lady in her bed."

He eyed Fiske accusingly. "If there were valuables in that

satchel, Mr. Fiske, why didn't you look after 'em yourself? Seems odd you'd put Miss Fortune to such a risk."

"I considered it best," Fiske said shortly.

Amos Decker spoke testily. "We better take a look around instead of palaverin' here all night."

"Exactly," Fiske said. "Although it likely will be only a waste of time. Whoever it was is probably out of reach."

So this was the stand they were taking. They certainly knew it was Susan who had filched the satchel and had passed it over to Kirby Dean.

Amos Decker brought more lanterns. The men hunted through the brush around the station. On the part of Amos Decker and his hostler and the two prospectors the search was in earnest, but for the others it was only a pretense.

It was one of the prospectors who came upon Fiske's leather satchel. It lay in the brush near the marsh and had been slashed open with a knife. It was empty!

Fiske slammed it on the ground. "Everything taken!" he raged. "Everything. Money! Business papers!"

Again he was only feigning anger and despair, Mike decided.

They carried on the mockery of a search until Fiske called a halt. "It's hopeless," he said. "Perhaps we can find something definite when daylight comes."

They returned to the station and everyone settled down for what rest they could get during the short remainder of the night.

Mike carried his pallet and blankets out of the station. "It's a little stuffy in here," he said.

He made his bed at a distance from the building, choosing a place under the mesquite trees. The ground was carpeted with dry seed pods from last year's crop and with brittle twigs, all of which crackled at a touch. These would give warning if anyone tried to approach.

Kirby Dean joined him, lugging his pallet. "Mind if I sleep here too?" he asked.

"Help yourself," Mike said, "provided you don't object to having a few scorpions for bedfellows. Or maybe a tarantula or a sidewinder."

"Better'n some other playmates I could mention," Dean said. "Thanks for slammin' that door, McLish. It saved my skin. I almost got what Calhoun gave that fellow at Fresno."

"You're as poor an actor as your lady friend," Mike said.

74

"You keep forgetting that fake southern accent when you're excited."

"Both Sue and I are new at this business," Dean sighed. "But it doesn't make much difference any longer. Fiske and his crowd likely guessed right from the start that Sue wasn't what she pretended. And they've suspected me too all the time. Now they're sure."

"What did you find in Fiske's satchel?" Mike asked.

"Nothing," Dean said.

Mike's head came up. "Nothing? What do you mean—nothing?"

"Nothing but a wad of newspapers. I went through 'em to make sure they were worthless and threw them away in the brush."

Mike lay silent for a time. "So it *was* a setup!" he said.

"Yeah," Dean said wearily. "They led Sue and me on like a pair of chumps. They tricked us into showing our hands. If they weren't sure before as to why we're traveling with this stage they damned well are now."

"In addition to that it gave them a chance to get rid of you," Mike said.

"That," Dean shrugged, "must have been strictly Calhoun's idea. I don't believe Fiske is a man to have a part in outright bushwhacking."

Mike lay back. Dean appeared to be engagingly frank. But only one thing had been proved. It was no longer reasonable to think that he and Susan might be secretly in league with Fiske, but that brought it all down to the money. That still seemed to be their sole objective.

Dean spoke. "Maybe Fiske sent the stuff by some other means. By mail, perhaps."

"If he did then it could still be with us in those bags we've had under our feet," Mike said. "I doubt that. I don't believe Fiske would trust anything like that to the mails through the Apache country."

There was only one other supposition, though Mike didn't mention it. The display of the satchel and the chain and lock probably had been a stage setting to divert attention from the real carrier. That carrier could be Calhoun. Or more likely, Julia Fortune.

Dean was silent for so long Mike believed he had fallen asleep. But he spoke again. "Watch out for Calhoun, McLish.

75

He's got no use for you. He came within an ace of putting a bullet in you tonight."

"And the same goes for you," Mike said. "He's only waiting for another chance to crowd you again."

"He'll soon get that chance," Dean said.

"You're still a fool," Mike said.

"I had my reasons for backing down at the Bella Union," Dean said. "But everything's out in the open now."

"Not entirely," Mike observed.

After that they quit talking. Mike finally slept.

When daybreak came Fiske and Calhoun led a new search of the surroundings. Again it was only a pretense. In addition, their own activities of the previous night had laid a maze of footprints around the station that muddied any attempt at picking up a trail.

Mike and Kirby Dean went along with the pretext, and wandered through the brush. Mike came upon an area where pages from newspapers were windblown into the branches of the mesquite and willows near the marsh. The pages were from the Los Angeles *Star* of the same edition that Mike had bought at the Bella Union containing the account of the slugging of Roger Vickers.

That proved that the contents of the satchel must have been changed after their departure from Los Angeles, for that edition of the paper had just arrived as they were waiting to board the stage. Or, more likely, Fiske had made the substitution during the delay after Susan had fainted.

Either way it was virtually certain that the money and the papers were still with them.

Fiske kept up the pretense of great loss. He raged and fumed. He offered rewards. "I'll sue John Butterfield for every cent he has in the world," he told Amos Decker. "I call on all of these passengers to witness that I'm filing claim against Butterfield this instant. I'll fix the amount later."

Nevertheless he resumed the journey with Calhoun and Julia Fortune. "I've got other business that can't wait," he told Decker. "But you people will hear from me again, I promise you that."

It was a subdued group that rode eastward out of Vallecito with the freshened horses in harness. There were only the six of them now. The two prospectors had decided to lay over at Vallecito, saying they would wait until the Apache trouble had eased. Mike surmised that the truth was that the affair of the previous night had convinced them that they wanted no further association with such companions.

Mike dozed, making up for the loss of rest at Vallecito. At times he only pretended to drowse while he studied Fiske and his companions. He met Julia Fortune's eyes at times and knew that she was well aware of his observance.

All of them were showing the weariness of the trip, but the strain seemed greatest on her and Fiske. Her eyes were dark and larger against the further thinness of her features. It occurred to Mike that it was not physical hardship that was wearing on her. She was under great mental strain.

This was the first day of real heat and dust and blowing sand. They were advancing into the lower desert. The wild flowers gave way to the endless creosote brush which stretched in all directions to the horizons. Its foliage greasily caught the glint of the sun.

Sand spumed up from hoofs and wheels. The wind carried it, holding them in a suffocating cloud, for it was a following wind. Susan and Julia Fortune protected their faces with doubled veils. The men tied neckerchiefs around their faces, so that they could have passed as a collection of bandits.

Susan and Julia accepted the driver's invitation to ride on the box where they woudl escape some of the dust. But the arid wind increased to a gale that kicked up a stinging sandstorm. This drove them back into the dubious shelter of the interior of the coach.

The wind died at sundown. At the Indian Wells stop they ate boiled salt pork, biscuits strong with soda, and coffee gritty with sand. The stationmaster, Pablo Gonzales, a jovial *Californiano* who possessed a big voice and a sizeable stomach, considered himself quite a man with the ladies. He was particularly taken with Susan. She tried to smile wanly at his jest, which reduced Pablo himself to a state of helpless laughter.

"You seem to be well acquainted with that unwashed Lothario," she said accusingly to Mike after she had escaped from Pablo's attentions.

"Pablo? Yes. In fact I was the one who hired him for that job when I was with Butterfield. He's been at Indian Wells ever since. Good man. Knows horses."

"Better than he knows women, though he's unaware of it," she said. "You're acquainted with the oddest persons. I noticed that he had considerable to say to you. He wasn't telling you any of his stale jokes. At least he wasn't giving out with that braying that he uses for laughter."

She was trying to draw from him the news Pablo had passed along. It had not been good news. The Apache outbreak, Pablo had said, was increasing. *"Muy malo!"* Pablo had termed it. Very bad!

Mike parried her try for information. He later took up the matter with Fiske and Calhoun.

"The ladies ought to make up their minds to turn back," he said. "They shouldn't go beyond Tucson at least. It'd be better if they went back to Los Angeles at least. Tucson's little more than an Indian village and Fort Yuma isn't much better. Pablo says that the most of the soldiers have been pulled out of Yuma."

"Thank you," Fiske said. "You may be right."

Calhoun thanked him also. But that was all. It was their way of telling him they intended to make their own decisions.

Mike talked to Kirby Dean. "If you can drive any sense into Miss Lang's head," he said, "tell her it won't be long until her hair will be mighty unsafe. She ought to head back on the next westbound stage."

"If we meet one," Dean said. "Pablo tells me none have come through for three days. But Julia Fortune seems to intend to keep going."

"I guess they're shooting for something so big they figure it's worth risking even her life for," Mike said.

"Then I'll never get Sue to quit either. She's as hard to budge as a Missouri mule."

"On that," Mike said, "we agree. But even mules can be reasoned with."

"You're welcome to try," Dean said. "I wish you luck. I'll watch."

"If necessary," Mike said, "I'll use force."

"I'll bind your wounds." Dean said.

"If you're still around," Mike answered.

Dean did not answer. He knew what Mike meant. He was again inviting Vance Calhoun's wrath by paying attention to Julia Fortune.

Mike had seen Julia looking at him at times, almost appealingly, as though hoping he would intervene. The fear was growing in her. Fiske, still preoccupied with his own plans, seemed unconcerned by Dean's brashness. In Fiske was a tolerance and even the air of a man who understood and sympathized with the infatuation.

But Calhoun's anger was now seething hot and unquenchable. He was biding his time, Mike decided. Dean was forcing the issue and Calhoun was only waiting the proper time to meet it.

Susan Lang's attitude was the real puzzle. Plainly, she was aware of what was brewing. If she held any bitterness toward Julia Fortune for being the cause of this situation it was not evident. There was a dread in her and almost a panic, as though she was racking her mind futilely for some plan which would stop this thing.

It came to a boil when they moved to resume their places in the coach after the stop at Alamo Mocho. Nightfall had come. Dean offered his hand to Julia as she prepared to enter the coach. Calhoun stepped up and pushed him roughly back. It was a repetition of the scene at the Bella Union.

"You've been warned that your attentions weren't wanted by Miss Fortune," Calhoun said.

"We'll let Miss Fortune decide that," Dean said.

Fiske again tried to intervene. "This is my affair, Vance," he said. "I'll take care of it."

Calhoun pushed him back, almost contemptuously. "This fellow hid back of petticoats at the Bella Union," Calhoun said. "He can't get away with that again."

Kirby Dean's face was gray and grim. "That's a blot on my conscience that I aim to remove," he said. "I no longer believe Miss Fortune is engaged to Fiske, or to anyone else. I also had other reasons for backing off at the Bella Union. They no longer exist."

Calhoun bowed formally. "I'm at your service."

"Am I the injured party, or are you?" Dean asked. "I'm not up on procedure in these bloodlettings. I understand you're better informed."

"Stop it!" Julia implored. "Stop it!"

But it was Susan Lang's face that Mike was seeing above all. She was ashen, deep tragedy in her eyes.

Mike spoke. "If it's fighting you two want you'll likely get your fill soon enough. I have a hunch the Apaches will take care of it."

Dean ignored that. "I prefer pistols," he said. "If that's all right with you, Calhoun."

"Very satisfactory," Calhoun said. "Very."

Dean was steady of voice, but Mike saw a gray and forlorn knowledge in his eyes. He knew that he was overmatched, but his pride drove him.

79

He spoke to Mike. "I'd appreciate it if you'd arrange the details."

Susan turned suddenly, hurried to the coach, and climbed in. She wanted to hide any display of emotion, Mike realized.

He was suddenly furious at Kirby Dean. "It'll be good riddance if Calhoun puts a bullet in you," he exploded. "There're some things you don't deserve."

Dean was taken aback by Mike's wrath, and bewildered.

Calhoun spoke. "We'll reach Fort Yuma about daybreak. That will be a good place. Daybreak is the customary time to settle matters of this kind. Will you act for me, Wheeler?"

"I'll have nothing to do with it," Fiske said wearily. "I want you and Mr. Dean to shake hands and forget it. All of this has been a mistake."

Calhoun shrugged. "I'll act in my own behalf." He turned to Mike. "Since your friend seems to prefer pistols I have the choice of distance. Thirty paces."

"Thirty!" Mike exclaimed. "Sixty steps between you? That's fifty yards."

An experienced marksman would have an advantage at that range, long for a pistol. And Calhoun evidently was experienced.

Calhoun smiled. "I'm sure your friend is safe at any distance. He won't show up to give me the satisfaction."

"I forbid this duel," Fiske said.

"You forbid it," Calhoun said scornfully.

He offered his arm to Julia, but she refused it and walked to the coach.

They rode in silence toward Fort Yuma, the coach lights casting grotesque shadows among the thorned growth alongside the trail. A coyote loped abreast of the coach, and continued to keep pace with it.

It was a display of playfulness and curiosity, a desire to match strength with this wheeled object which roared along so noisily, this swift wagon. Mike had seen this trait before in wild creatures—deer and antelope and even the wary gray wolf.

Calhoun drew his pistol and killed the coyote in its tracks. In that light the shot from a moving vehicle at a running target demonstrated his skill with a weapon for Kirby Dean's benefit. Calhoun holstered the weapon and sat back, a trifle self-conscious at making this demonstration of vanity, but pleased also with its success.

Kirby Dean gave no sign that he had noticed, although the report of the gun had struck a hard blow at the nerves of all of them.

CHAPTER TEN

They arrived at Cook's Wells shortly before midnight. Dean and Susan walked away while the fresh team was being brought up from the corral. She had a hand linked in his arm. They were not talking, but it was evident that they wanted to spend this moment together.

Julia came to where Mike was smoking a stogie. Again she wanted to talk with him alone. She waited until Mike had walked with her out of hearing of the others.

"This duel must be stopped," she said.

When Mike didn't speak, she sighed. "I know you blame me. I blame myself. I tried to discourage Kirby Dean. I really tried."

"Yes," Mike said. "I'm sure you did. This isn't your fault. It's out of your hands."

"Mr. Dean was right," she said. "I'm not engaged to marry Mr. Fiske. I never was. Wheeler said that so as to keep them from fighting that night in Los Angeles."

Mike nodded. "Everybody has figured it that way. Dean was fooled for a while but when he got over the shock he knew you had gone along with it so as to protect him from Calhoun."

"Yes. And that made it worse. Now it's his pride, his hellish, stubborn pride that's driving him into this."

Mike eyed her. "Would it really matter if anything happened to him?"

"If you're asking if I might be learning to care for him that's not a fair question," she said.

"Just what is Fiske to you?" Mike asked.

She debated that so long he believed she wasn't going to answer. Finally she spoke. "He was in love with my mother when he was a young man. She jilted him and ran away with a handsome, worthless man. That man was my father. He's dead. I never saw him. He never married my mother. She did not live long. She died of heartbreak and disgrace. All of this happened in the East. Wheeler Fiske saw to it that I was educated- in private schools. I had some talent as a singer. He encouraged that. He came to California during the gold rush. He brought me there after I had finished my schooling. Against his wishes I went on the stage."

"You don't really need to tell me all this," Mike said.

"You're the first person in a long time I've felt like explaining anything to," she said. "I've seen pictures of my mother. I look very much like her, but I'm not as attractive."

"In that case she must have been a real stunner."

"Wheeler never married," she said. "After I grew up he thought he was in love with me. He was only trying to live his life over. He realized that it was the memory of my mother he was still in love with. And he still is."

She gazed up at Mike. "And I love him and respect him. But only as I would a father. I owe him so very much, I'll never turn against him. I want you to understand that. No matter if he might be wrong I'll stand by him."

"That sounds like a warning," Mike said.

She didn't respond to that. "I have the death of one man on my conscience," she said.

"What?"

"He was killed in one of those damnable affairs of honor. That was six years ago when I was nineteen. I was the cause, just as I'm the cause this time."

She gave him a bitter smile. "I'm sure you know that I'm not exactly a puritanical person. I've enjoyed life. I've had my share of romances. I'm twenty-five years old. But I couldn't stand having—having Kirby Dean killed because of me. He has no chance against Calhoun."

"Any man with a gun in his hand and sand in his gizzard has a chance," Mike said.

"I'm sure Susan Lang is also anxious to stop this duel," Julia said. "Very anxious. Has she asked you to help her?"

"Why do you say that?" Mike demanded.

"I have my reasons. They're not the strangers they pretended to be when Susan boarded the coach at Fresno. Let's be frank. We both know why they're aboard this coach and what they're after. They're very close to each other."

"*Were* very close, maybe," Mike said.

"You mean that I came between them?"

"That's the size of it," Mike said bluntly. "You're right about Susan. She's upset about this duel. Plenty. But why would she ask me to help?"

"For the same reason I came to you. There's nobody else to turn to. Kirby Dean must be left behind—forcibly, if necessary."

"He isn't as helpless as you seem to believe," Mike said. "Nor Miss Lang."

"As for Miss Lang," Julia said, "I'm sure of that."

The coach was ready to pull out. Mike handed Julia aboard. He had promised nothing. She had taken his silence as a refusal. She sat in the shadows, apparently asleep, but he was sure she was awake.

Susan, at Mike's side, was not asleep either. She leaned close, her lips brushing his ear. "What did Julia want of you?" she murmured.

"She asked a small favor," Mike answered. "Kirby Dean's life. She seems to think she's responsible if Calhoun kills him."

"She's exactly right," Susan said fiercely. "He's bedazzled by her."

"And neglecting you?" Mike asked.

"Neglecting me?" She sat up straight, and he saw that she was glaring angrily at him in the darkness.

But she withheld whatever was in her mind, perhaps because, like Mike, she realized that others might be straining to hear what they were saying. But she continued to sit rigid and aloof from him.

It still lacked two hours until daybreak when the coach reached the Pilot Knob swing station, the last stop before Fort Yuma. Insects wheeled in the lantern light. A lizzard darted underfoot. Beetles crept in the dust.

The two men in the station crew were on edge and heavily armed. Just before dark they had gone through a touchy session with a dozen Yuma Indians who had been of a mind to help themselves to the horses in the corral. The Yumas had vanished after a few shots had been fired.

"All the tribes are gittin' bold," the station keeper told Mike. "But you likely won't have any trouble between here an' the fort, bein' as you'll be ridin' in the dark all the way to the river. Them Yumas don't like to be wanderin' around at night."

Susan Lang made sure it was Mike who helped her alight from the coach. Her hand held him back while the others trooped into the station.

"We've got to do something," she whispered. "We can't let Dean fight that man and be killed."

"What would you suggest?" Mike asked.

"There's only one way. He must be left here when the stage pulls out."

"Now that's a coincidence," Mike said. "Julia Fortune made the same suggestion. Are you asking me to use violence?"

"Better a broken jaw than a coffin," she said. She glanced around. "There seems to be some sort of a stable or building out there in the darkness. That should be far enough away. You can wait there and I'll walk with him in that direction. You'll have to find something to tie him up with."

She added anxiously, "You'll be careful when you hit him, won't you?"

"Hit him?" Mike demanded. "With what?"

"Your fist, of course. We only want to stun him, not maim him. Don't tell me you don't know how to swing a fist. Not with that face of yours. You'll have to arrange with the station men to take care of him after we're gone."

"Your solicitude for him is touching," Mike said. "And what about the main purpose of this trip? I believe that you were sent to steal certain items from Wheeler Fiske. I believe that is more important that interfering in Dean's romantic troubles. Or am I wrong?"

"Wrong," she said. "I haven't forgotten the other matter, but Dean's life comes first. In addition I need his help."

"Any idea where these items might be?" Mike asked.

"It could be in their baggage," she said.

"That's what I've been thinking."

"We'll have to search it," she said. "You'll have to arrange a delay at Fort Yuma so as to give us a little time."

"Who'll do this searching?" Mike demanded.

She glared at him. "I assumed that you might risk your hide to that extent at least. You still don't have any confidence in me, do you?"

"I don't aim to be set up for a clay pigeon like Roger Vickers was in that house in San Francisco," Mike said. "If Kirby Dean doesn't plug me for trying to waylay him here at Pilot Knob I might stand a good chance of getting it when I do this ransacking of other people's belongings at Yuma."

She was wide-eyed. "Wait a minute! Are you accusing me of betraying Roger Vickers?"

"I was the one who carried Vickers out of that house that night," Mike said. "Someone had taken a shot at me. I believe it was the same Murdock who tried it again at Fresno.

I had gone back to the house to warn Vickers about something I had found out. I was too late. They had already tried to murder him."

"You—you mean you knew all the time that he had been hurt? All during the trip to Los Angeles? Why didn't you tell me?"

Mike eyed her, puzzled. It was as though she felt he was guilty of some unpardonable piece of indifference.

He drew from his pocket the white cloth star, holding it spread on his palm so that only she could see, for Calhoun was standing in the door of the station gazing speculatively in their direction.

"Do you remember this?" he asked.

She gazed blankly at first at the star which was becoming frayed and slightly tattered. Her expression changed.

"I see that you do," Mike said triumphantly. "I found it in the room where you lived in that house. I saw the flag Dean carried that started a secession riot that night in the plaza."

He peered closer at her. "You double-crossed Vickers, didn't you? You and Dean don't give a damn about secession or the Union. All you're after is the money."

"You can believe what you please," she breathed, her teeth set in anger. "I'll never tell you how wrong you are. But you're wrong. So terribly wrong. We've wasted enough time. Calhoun is wondering what we're mumbling about. I'll lead Dean into your hands as soon as I get the sign from you that you're ready."

"Do you think I'm going through with this?" Mike demanded.

"Yes," she sniffed. "But because Julia Fortune asked you. She seems to have you dangling at her finger tips like she has Dean."

She walked away. The hell of it, Mike reflected, was that she was right. He was going through with it. But not because of Julia Fortune, although she was a factor. The truth was that he still could not make up his mind as to where Susan Lang stood in all of this.

He talked to the station keeper, a bearded man named Pete Rice, whom Amos Decker had said could be trusted. Pete Rice had received the order to give Mike anything he wanted and therefore listened attentively.

"After we pull out, you might find a man tied up back of the blacksmith shed," Mike said. "I'll need some rope to hobble him. You can turn him loose after we're well on our way. He'll probably be pretty mad and will want to follow us. Discourage him. Keep him here as long as you can."

Pete Rice furnished him with lengths of braided rawhide hackamore line. Mike hid these under his coat. He let Susan know that he was prepared, then drifted away, circled the shed, and waited there in darkness.

It wasn't long before he heard Susan and Dean approaching. "What good is it going to do to talk to McLish?" Dean was muttering. "I know what he'll say. He's already said it."

"What he has to tell you is for your own good," Susan answered. "He may be a little slow of wit and suspicious of anything he doesn't clearly understand, but alongside of you he's a man of brilliant intellect. This duel is a piece of complete insanity."

Mike stepped into view. "I'll be brief," he said to Dean. "Do you see that man over there, watching us?"

Dean fell for the moth-worn trap. He turned, gazing in the direction Mike was pointing.

"This is for your own good," Mike said.

His fist landed to the base of the jaw where its stunning effect was maximum and its lasting damage slight. Dean went down, floundering and dazed.

Mike leaped on him, binding his wrists and ankles. Susan, in a dither of apprehension, kneeled, stroking Dean's hair. "I hope you didn't hit him too hard!" she chattered.

"It's my knuckles I'm worrying about," Mike snorted. "That was like taking a whack at solid rock."

Dean began to gurgle. Mike thrust in his mouth a gag that Susan provided. "It's for your own good," she whispered. "Go back to San Francisco. Don't blame McLish. This was my idea."

She added, "And Julia's, if that's any consolation to you."

She and Mike left him there, still mumbling and struggling, for the driver was yelling impatiently for all passengers to climb aboard.

"I'll have a brawl on my hands if he ever catches up with me," Mike said. "He's not the forgiving kind."

The others were already seated when they entered the coach. The driver counted noses, then peered around. "Where's the other feller?" he asked Susan. "The towheaded one?"

"He isn't coming," Susan said. "He's decided to stay over."

"He might have give me a leetle notice," the driver grumbled. He climbed to the box and they were on their way.

Calhoun laughed loudly, derisively. "I told you that you were wasting your worry on him, McLish," he said. "He's crawled out of it again."

"It might be possible to arrange a substitute," Mike said.

Calhoun's amusement ended abruptly. "Namely?" he asked.

Susan spoke quickly. "It's ended. Let it rest there."

"Miss Lang is right," Fiske said. "Let's tend to our own knitting, Vance."

In Fiske was an uncertainty and even a trace of deference toward Calhoun. A change had taken place in their relationship. Fiske was no longer sure of his grip on the reins and seemed to be afraid of the direction the chariot he had set in motion was now taking. He had dark circles under his eyes, and the lines of weariness were deeper around his mouth.

Calhoun gazed at him, and Mike again saw contempt there. Calhoun decided against following up the matter. "As you wish, Wheeler," he said. To Mike he said, "Some other time, perhaps."

Susan sighed and sank back in her seat. She leaned against Mike. The strain of the miles since San Francisco apparently struck her all at once. She was suddenly sleeping exhaustedly. Mike placed an arm around her and supported her as the coach lurched over the sandy desert trail.

CHAPTER ELEVEN

They were all aroused from their tired sleep at dawn by the report of a cannon.

"Fort Yuma," Mike said. "That's the morning gun."

Susan sat up, blinking, trying to drive away the cobwebs. Her eyes were soft, color high in her cheeks. She said, "You've got sand in your eyebrows, Mike McLish."

"And in my teeth," Mike said. "And in my ears. There must be half a ton of it aboard. Most of it in our clothes. That stretch of road was laid out by the devil himself."

"I've heard," she remarked, "that you had much to do with building this portion of Butterfield."

"For that, you'll be sentenced to eat beef as tough as bootleather and coffee that'll taste like it was boiled in that same boot," Mike declared.

Julia Fortune spoke. "The sentence will begin at once. Here's the stage station. It looks just like all the others. Ugly."

The station stood near the army post on a bluff overlooking the river.

"I had visions of being met by handsome army officers," Susan said.

"There ain't much left of the army around here, miss," the station master told her. "There's only a corporal an' a handful of men at the post. The rest has gone back East to give what-fer to the secess if they git gay."

Fiske spoke. "What news have you heard from the East, my friend?"

"Looks like real trouble as sure as little apples. Abe Lincoln says he's goin' to show 'em who's boss. He ain't goin' to stand fer bustin' up the Union after he's inaugurated. Thet'll be tomorrow."

"Tomorrow?" Mike exclaimed. He had lost track of the days.

"Lincoln won't have anything to say about it," Fiske snapped. "He'll have to accept the fact that the South is forming a separate nation. If he doesn't he'll have only himself to blame for the consequences."

The stationmaster bristled. He was a leathery beanpole of a man named Cass Bidwell. "Mister, if'n you rebs want a fight you're goin' to git yore bellyful of it."

Fiske had grown irascible along with his weariness and was ready to push the issue, but Calhoun stalled it off by brushing him into the background.

"Just what've you heard from the East?" Calhoun asked Bidwell. "We've had no news since leaving Los Angeles, and damned little there."

"Then you know all I know," Bidwell said. "Stages ain't comin' through too regular lately. The people aboard 'em has been too busy worryin' about 'Paches an' their own skins than to keep track of a lot of hotheads way back there. This secession business won't amount to much anyway. Abe Lincoln'll send a couple companies o' troops down there an' throw all them rebs in the calaboose."

Even Fiske joined Calhoun in smiling bleakly, but both decided there was no point in clashing with Bidwell.

"Have any more states seceded?" Mike asked.

"Last I heerd, which was five days ago, Virginny was still on the fence," Bidwell said. "Them folks in Virginny ought to have better sense than to git mixed up in this foolishness."

"What about Tennessee?" Calhoun demanded. "And Arkansas?"

"How would I know, mister? Even the army post ain't had word for days. There's no telegraph line through this country. Nobody knows what'n blazes is goin' on back East."

Mike finished breakfast ahead of the others and strolled out. He found Cass Bidwell struggling with paperwork in the little cubbyhole in the station that served as an office.

Mike closed the door. "I'm Mike McLish of Central Overland," he said. "Does that mean anything to you?"

Bidwell grinned and shifted his cud of tobacco. "Yup! I figgered you was him. A general order come through a couple days ago from San Francisco to roll out the red carpet fer you if you showed up. They sent a description o' you. An' I happen to know you by reputation. Shake."

They shook hands. "First," Mike said, "I'm passing word down the line to be ready to cut it for California with everything you can lay hands on if the order to abandon comes through. Stations west of here will be trying to stock up on fodder. Grab onto any you can scare up yourself and haul it with you if possible. There'll be a lot of livestock coming through. And people too. You'll need extra grub."

"If the johnnycakes don't grab the fodder an' livestock first," Bidwell grunted.

"What have you really heard?" Mike asked.

"Not much more'n I told the old turkey buzzard out there. He's Wheeler Fiske, ain't he? I knew him when I worked in the Los Angeles station a year back. Secess to the core. All I git air rumors. By the dozen. Country's full of 'em. But I gather that there's some fire to all the smoke. The fellers on the other side of the fence has got the same idea of gittin' their hands on Butterfield."

"Any line on how they aim to do it?"

"Drivers an' passengers comin' through last week said a lot of tough strangers had showed up around El Paso an' in the Mesilla Valley durin' the past month or so. They was still driftin' in, last I heard."

"Armed?"

"They had supply wagons an' was well heeled with rifles an' sidearms. They stacked up like men who knew how to shoot."

"Uniformed?"

"Nope. Rough-dressed. But somebody's gatherin' 'em up an' it's certain they aim to head west. Maybe they figger on takin' California. If so they won't overlook the chance to grab Butterfield."

Mike stood frowning. Evidently Roger Vickers' information had been correct. Fiske's plan was already in operation. His invasion force was already being assembled, or perhaps completed.

"I want these passengers delayed here a few hours," Mike said. "Long enough to be separated from their baggage. I want to take a look at some of it. You can tell them the coach needs repairs. A busted pole or a brace. Anything."

"I kin do better'n that," Bidwell said. "I'll have to lay 'em over here awhile anyway. I've got orders not to use any more of the big Concords east o' here. From now on, through the 'Pache country you travel in mudwagons. Furthermore, there ain't any mudwagon here. One was supposed to have come in from Tucson last night but a rider rode through today, sayin' it wouldn't git here 'til this afternoon. I take it thet it's Fiske you're after. I wouldn't mind seein' his baggage mussed up."

"I might also look at the stuff belonging to the dark-haired lady with him," Mike said. "And also that of the other man, Vance Calhoun."

"Calhoun?" Bidwell repeated. "There's a feller around here who's been askin' if anybody named Calhoun had come through by stage lately."

Mike came to attention. "What does he look like?"

"Hard formation, if you ask me. He looks familiar, at that. I've seen him somewhere before, but can't place him. He showed up three or four days ago. He's been hangin' out at Arizona City, which is thet hellhole you can see about a mile down the river if you step outside. Said he'd been prospectin' up in the desert, but a driver told me he was certain he had sighted the feller five days ago, east of here an' headin' this way saddleback. He walks down here to the station each time a stage pulls in. Fact is, here he comes right now."

A heavy-set, thick-legged man appeared on foot in front of the station. Calhoun was still at breakfast in the adjoining room. The arrival started to enter the eating room, then changed his mind. He came to the office and tapped on the door.

Bidwell looked at Mike inquiringly. When Mike nodded, Bidwell admitted the man.

"Howdy," the arrival said. "I've decided to buy fare as far as El Paso, mister. It looks like there's room on this stage."

"Your friend Calhoun just pulled in," Bidwell said. "He's in there eatin' breakfast."

The man looked surprised. "He is? I didn't see him."

"He's the younger one of the two with the ladies," Mike said. "The one with the brown hair."

"Oh," the man said. "That ain't my friend. The world's full of Calhouns. It's Fred Calhoun I was hoping to see. Me and him were goin' to do some prospectin', but I reckon he's given up the idea or something's happened to him. At least I can't hang around here any longer, waitin'."

Bidwell nodded. "But this run won't pull out until the coach from Tucson pulls in. That likely won't be until sometime this afternoon. Where'll you be?"

"At the settlement. At the cantina."

"I'll send word. Pay for your ticket now, if you want the seat held. Other fares might show up."

"Sure," the man said, and produced a wallet.

He wore the dress of a prospector—blue cotton shirt, woolen pants stuffed into hide boots, a round-brimmed felt hat. The clothes were fairly new and did not seem exactly in keeping with his character. Nor did his speech, which varied from crudeness to that of a man of fair education. He had wide, heavy jaws which were closely shaven to a blue-black cast. His eyes were Indian black.

Mike returned to the eating room and filled his coffee tin again. Susan sat apart from the others. She seemed depressed. Mike decided that it was best to stay away from her.

Fiske looked gray and spent. Julia sat with him. Mike heard her say, "You must get some rest, Wheeler. You need that more than anything else."

"We lost a full day at Vallecito," Fiske said, his voice sharp with strain. "Now this. Confound it! If I only knew what was going on! If I could only find out what's happening at Montgomery! And at Washington!"

Vance Calhoun seemed undisturbed and even mockingly bored by Fiske's state of nerves. "How about a stroll, Julia?" he said. "It will do you good."

There was calculated impertinence in the way he used her name. Mike saw Fiske stiffen as though about to make an issue of it. Julia's hand on his arm restrained him.

She spoke without looking at Calhoun. "No, thank you."

Calhoun left the table, giving Julia a thin smile. Mike saw her wince. She was afraid of him.

The new passenger left Bidwell's office and walked away, heading on foot down the road toward a straggle of adobe structures that were visible along the river to the south. That would be the Arizona City that Bidwell had mentioned. It had the earmarks of the customary appendage to an army post.

Presently Calhoun, riding a saddled pony which he must have borrowed from Bidwell, passed by and also headed for the settlement.

A sudden, startling thought came to Mike. He hurried back to the office.

"What name did the new passenger give?" he asked Bidwell.

"Signed under the name of Bill Jackson," Bidwell said. He paused to give importance to his next words. "But his real name is Durkin. Lew Durkin. The Regulator. I reckon you've heard o' him? An' them?"

"Are you sure?" Mike demanded.

"I didn't recognize him at first. It's been half a dozen years since I had got a look at him, an' then not too close a peek. He was thinner then an' wore a black beard. He used to come

93

into a town where I worked with a livery outfit. Him an'
some of his Regulators came there at times to drink an'
gamble. It's him as sure as there's fuzz on a peach. I got a
close look at him just now with a shadow across his face
that made him look like he was wearin' a beard. I knew
I'd seen him somewhere in the past. It came to me so sudden
I almost give it away. He's Lew Durkin."

"I just had the same hunch," Mike snapped.

He stepped outside and peered. Calhoun had overtaken
Durkin and had loped on past him and into the settlement.
Durkin, on foot, was now nearing the buildings.

"Have you got another saddle-horse?" Mike asked Bidwell.

"Nope. Only a couple o' wild Spanish mules. You'd be
better off on foot."

"Blast it!" Mike fumed. "Listen! Pass the word to Miss
Lang that she'll have to take care of searching the baggage."

Bidwell gulped. "Miss Lang? Which one's her?"

"The one with the lighter-colored hair."

"Thet purty gray-eyed susie?" Bidwell protested. "Do you
mean she's helpin' you? Now, McLish, if Lew Durkin's mixed
up in this, it's no place for the likes of her or any woman.
They say Durkin made a speciality of mistreatin' women. Him
an' his Regulators."

"But Durkin hasn't got his Regulators with him now,"
Mike said. "In addition, it's necessary."

Bidwell shrugged dubiously. "It's your funeral, I reckon.
Or hers. I'll move the baggage an' mail into the blacksmith
shed an' lock it in while we're waitin'. I'll give her the key.
She'll have to figger out a way to sneak out there when the
others ain't lookin'."

"If I spoke to her myself Fiske or the others might catch
on," Mike said. "So it's up to you."

Bidwell sighed. "You're the kind that breeds trouble, Mc-
Lish. It's writ all over you. An' this Miss Lang looks like
she's cut from the same shingle. She's purty as apple pie.
But she's spunky. Plenty."

Mike set out on foot for Arizona City. He lengthened his
stride without trying to appear in too much of a hurry, for
he was visible on that flat stretch of road from both the
station and the settlement.

He felt that his walk was useless, but it was worth a try.
Lew Durkin's presence here needed explanation. Roger Vickers had said that Lew Durkin was in charge of organizing
the invading force in Texas for Fiske, but under another name.

Fiske evidently had never met Durkin personally for he had shown no interest in the man.

Yet, Durkin must have come to Fort Yuma for the sole purpose of meeting Calhoun and that purpose had been important enough to keep him waiting for days.

Their conference likely was taking place right at this moment, for Durkin had reached the settlement and vanished among the buildings. But Fiske was being kept in the dark.

The mile distance seemed endless to Mike. The sun was up and beginning to blaze down. His boots became tight on his feet. He carried his coat.

He finally made it to the straggle of adobe and slab buildings. The cantina was the nucleus of the dusty settlement. The huts of Indians, with walls made of reeds, and grass roofs, formed a background. Brown children scurried around. Mexican and Indian women boldly ogled him and made comments.

The horse Calhoun had been riding stood at the rail in front of the cantina. Mike entered the place. The interior was gloomy after the diamond brightness of the outside sun.

Calhoun sat at one of the two card tables, toying with a cup of mescal. Lew Durkin stood at the bar, a similar drink before him. He was shaking dice in a leather cup. A peon in a poncho dozed in a heelsquat against a wall. The only other person present was the *cantinero* who was playing dice with Durkin.

It was all too casual, too staged. Mike could see other wet glass rings on the poker table and knew that Durkin had been sitting there also. He and Calhoun had had their heads together and had been aware of Mike's approach and had parted before he arrived.

Mike went to the bar. Only mescal, the fiery lightning in a bottle that was distilled from the juice of the maguey, and pulque, the bitter beer from the same source, were available.

Mike choose the lesser of the two evils. "Something to wash the dust from the throat, *amigo*," he said to the *cantinero*. "The beer, if it is cool."

It was fairly cool. He tasted it and winced. Lew Durkin spoke jovially. "My name's Jackson. Bill Jackson. I'm travelin' east when the stage pulls out. You're a passenger too, I reckon. We might as well get acquainted."

"McLish," Mike said. "Mike McLish."

The hand Durkin offered was powerful. At close range he was impressive. There was a stone-hard quality in his beefy face and sharp intelligence in his dark eyes. Beneath his affability was truculence and arrogance. Here was a ruthless individual.

Durkin motioned to Calhoun. "This round's on me, friend. I reckon you two know each other, having come in on the same stage."

Calhoun joined them and seemed willing to call a truce. "Yes," he said. "We've traveled a long way together. To your health, Mr. Jackson."

Mike bought a round of refreshments in his turn. If Calhoun held any animosity toward him he seemed to continue to be willing to let it rest, at least for the time being.

Mike stayed in the cantina, sitting in a chair, his legs resting on a table. Calhoun and Lew Durkin played euchre.

He wondered if Susan had found a chance to search the baggage. With Calhoun out of the way she at least would have had only Fiske and Julia to worry about.

The cantina, squalid as it was, certainly was cooler and more comfortable than the stage station. Occasionally he ordered another cup of pulque. It was a drink with which he had become accustomed in former days. Once his tongue got used to it again its appeal was reviving.

He was thinking of the night in the shabby house when Roger Vickers had speculated on the possibility that San Francisco could be seized and looted by guerrillas if they were properly armed and organized.

At the time the thought had seemed fantastic. It no longer appeared farfetched. The stake Fiske had been playing for was enormous, but there was so reason why other men couldn't add to the pot and play a hand also. The deadly potentialities of the rift between the North and South had been driven home to Mike during this journey.

The Amos Deckers and the Cass Bidwells were loyal to the Union, but there were other stationmasters who would stand by the Confederacy. Some of these men were friends of Mike. Sincere men, who would fight for their beliefs. War was coming.

This was the sort of climate in which opportunists like Lew Durkin flourished. And Calhoun. Whatever message one of them had brought for the other had been passed before Mike could get within sight of them, before he could see or hear anything that might have given him a hint. The only thing sure was that whatever their plan, Wheeler Fiske was not included in it.

CHAPTER TWELVE

At midafternoon a blast from a brass horn aroused them. The stage from Tucson was pulling in. Mike, Durkin, and Calhoun headed back to the station. By the time they arrived, the vehicle was ready for the return trip. Spanish mules were in harness, and they were wild and only half-broken. The baggage was stored in the boot.

In the advertising put out by the stage company their new conveyance was grandly referred to as a "Celerity Coach." It was more commonly known as a mudwagon. That described it.

It was intensely practical. Its body was square and uncompromisingly homely in aspect. It had a top of treated canvas stretched over wooden struts. Its passengers were more exposed to the elements.

Like the bigger, gilded coaches which were too valuable to risk in Apache country, the mudwagon was of Abbot, Downing construction which meant that it was durable. Tough, lighter in weight than the Concords, and with a lower center of gravity, it had many advantages on mountain roads. Comfort of the passengers was not among these attributes.

There were no other passengers. Travel through Arizona had grown decidedly unpopular. Susan took Calhoun's place, sitting with Fiske and Julia. Something in her attitude told Mike that she had failed in the matter of the luggage search. That meant that with seven hundred miles of their journey behind them they still had no result to show.

She shot smoldering glances at him occasionally. She had a quarrel to pick with him, evidently, and was only biding her time.

In contrast, Durkin and Calhoun, who were Mike's seat-mates, were talkative and jovial. Mike also felt expansively mellow, and even traded quips with them.

He could see that this did not soften Susan's attitude toward him. Her hair needed combing. She kept angrily tucking away straying strands.

A smudge of dust stood on her forehead, of which she was unaware. She used a small hand mirror and finally discovered this blemish. She uttered a dismal groan and scrubbed at the spot with a kerchief. She gave Mike a glare of new intensity. She seemed to hold him personally responsible.

He tried to avoid her at the next swing stop, but she firmly took his arm and maneuvered him to where they could talk without being overheard.

"What luck?" he asked.

"A good question," she said grimly. "The answer, briefly, is—none. It isn't in their luggage."

"Then you did get a chance to search it?"

"I did. While you were swilling whatever vile liquor you found at that saloon, I was creeping around like a mole in that confounded blacksmith shed. You and those other two scoundrels smelled like distilleries all the way from Fort Yuma."

"You had trouble?" Mike asked.

"Trouble, he says. Mr. Bidwell locked the doors to make sure nobody would walk in on me while I searched. He left me there two hours. I had a lantern for light. There were no windows in the place. With the sun beating down on the roof it was like spending an afternoon in a good hot frying pan."

"I'm sorry. And you didn't find a thing?"

"Nothing except clothes. And more clothes."

"Could it have been in false bottoms?"

"I made sure there were none. Please give me a little credit for common sense. It just isn't there. But I know where it probably is."

"Julia Fortune?"

"Yes. I'm not the only one who seems to have done some sewing lately. I happen to know that Julia also did some needlework while we were at the Bella Union in Los Angeles. She was supposed to have been resting, but afterward, while we were having supper together, I noticed a little wad of thread clippings in the waste box."

"What does that mean?" Mike asked.

"You *are* dense, aren't you? Julia had pulled a lot of stitches out of some garment. It was a lining, according to the kind of thread I saw."

"And she stitched the lining up again with something added," Mike said. "Bonds and gold notes and papers. Just what sort of a garment would this be in your opinion?"

"A petticoat," she said. "Some of the very best ones, of satin, such as Julia wears, are lined."

Mike sighed. "This could be a problem."

"Your problem," she said.

"Why mine?"

"Julia thinks highly of you. I doubt if she would resent it if you paid a little more attention to her."

Mike glared. "You mean in a personal way, of course?"

"Any way to get your arm around her."

"I'll be teetotally damned!" Mike snorted. "Females are the most coldhearted, ruthless creatures on earth. You're telling me to make love to her so that I can find out if she's carrying what we want in her dress."

"Don't tell me you have scruples against that also," Susan sniffed. "I know better. I've seen the gleam in your eye when you've been talking to her. She's very attractive. And with a gorgeous figure."

"If I put my arm around a girl it's not to find out if she's stuffed with paper," Mike said.

"How vulgar you are!" she said. "Of course, I realize that you'd be inviting Mr. Calhoun's attention. You might be called out. Is that the way you say it? I wouldn't blame you for not wanting to be shot down like a dog in a duel."

"You're again trying to prod me into doing what you want me to do by saying I'm afraid," Mike said. "You just don't fight fair, do you? You gouge, scratch, kick or use any other kind of means that come handy, don't you? You'd probably even drive a hatpin into a man."

"Hatpin? Now hold on! Why did you bring that up?"

"I know you're still toting around those two skewers you had in that fool hat you got rid of at Fresno," Mike said.

"You—you—why I carry those hatpins on—on——"

"On your garter," Mike grinned.

"Oh, my!" she breathed, horrified. "How——"

"Keep calm," he said. "One of them jammed me in the leg the other night when you were sleeping on my shoulder."

"That's better," she said. "Not that I'm happy at sleeping on your shoulder. I didn't realize. I'm sorry."

"At least I found that *you* weren't stuffed with paper," Mike said.

"Let's drop that subject," she said. "We were talking about Julia Fortune, remember?"

"You're wrong about her," Mike said. "She can't be bought with a kiss or a few soft words. She's loyal to Fiske."

"Well, well! Has she confided in you? Did she tell you the story of her life?"

"Something like that," Mike said.

"And you believed her?"

"Yes, but I haven't got time to tell it all to you right now. We're ready to roll."

They walked to the mudwagon. The stationkeeper said, "Tucson tomorrow, folks. Ain't much of a place, but it's a crowd compared to what you'll see beyond."

They were hours behind schedule when the driver shouted, "Tucson!" He sounded his bugle.

Mike alighted, leaning against a bleak afternoon wind that rattled the spiny brush. Mountain ridges stood in funereal hues against the coming twilight. Tucson had even less to offer than Arizona City. Its scattered structures faded off into the hovels of Pima Indians.

"A rocky place to stay in," he said to Susan. "I doubt if there's half a dozen people here who can speak English. And there probably isn't another white woman within two hundred miles."

"Stay? Who's staying?"

"You," Mike said. "It isn't safe east of here. You know that."

"I'm not staying here," she said flatly. "I talked to the men at some of the swing stations last night. They said the Apache trouble seems to have died down. Stages are coming through again."

It was true. The stationkeeper at Tucson, Paddy O'Shay, said the Apaches seemed to have left their stamping grounds in the Chiricahua Mountains. At least no stages had met trouble in the past three days.

"But ye niver know what Cochise an' his cunnin' divils are up to or when they'll show up again," O'Shay said.

O'Shay was an ardent supporter of the secession. When he learned the identity of Wheeler Fiske his respect knew no bounds. He touched the brim of his hat each time he addressed Fiske.

"They've put Abe Lincoln in the White House, bad cess to them," he told Fiske. "Sure an' the inauguration was held, accordin' to word that came through only yesterday by stage. He made it plain, did Abe Lincoln, as to just where he stands. 'Tis war he's wantin'. The whole country below the Mason-Dixon line is seethin'. Who is Abe Lincoln to tell men what they can do an' what they can't do wid their own property?"

100

"It's coming," Fiske said. He was listless, almost sad. Mike believed that an uncertainty had entered his mind lately. Mike surmised that Fiske had hoped the matter could be settled without war.

Calhoun spoke. "And high time it came." Again there was scorn for Fiske in his attitude.

Fiske gazed at Calhoun as though never exactly having seen him before, then walked away, his hands clasped at his back, thinking.

Julia stood gazing after him. Mike, on an impulse, moved to her side. "United we stand," he murmured. "Divided, we fall."

That did it. Tears suddenly swam in her eyes. She was at the point of breaking down. Her hands gripped his arm hard, seeking support and strength. He turned her and walked her around the corner of the station, out of sight and hearing of the others. There she leaned against him, giving in to deep sobbing. He placed an arm around her, steadying her.

"Is he wrong?" she asked brokenly.

"Nothing is right that has to be settled by war," Mike said.

"Someday . . ." she began. "Someday. . . "

She did not finish it. It came to Mike that she did not believe in all the things Wheeler Fiske believed in. Her spirit was at its ebb. He sensed that if he asked her she might even surrender the money and the papers. He was suddenly certain that she was carrying them and had them with her at this moment.

He did not ask it. It didn't seem fair to her, unarmed as she was at the moment by her emotions.

She gained control of herself and drew back. "Thank you," she said.

"For what?"

"For not taking advantage of a moment of weakness," she said. "But that's over with. I'll never turn against him. He's been too kind to me to be treated like that."

She left him then. But she knew that he was after the papers and the money. She had also made her final decision. She must have been debating it in her mind for a long time. Her loyalty to Fiske was greater than her own beliefs. The material she carried could only be taken from her by force.

The stop was only long enough for a meal and to shift baggage to a new coach. This was a mudwagon also, but of far greater antiquity even than the one that had carried them from Fort Yuma. It needed paint. The spokes and fellies had the bone-gray look of long exposure to weather.

There were holes in the body and in the leather wings of the boot. Some of these had been patched. Mike saw that many had been made by bullets. Others by arrows, no doubt. Some were recent.

Calhoun and Durkin did not miss the significance of these souvenirs. They stood frowning, troubled. Fiske, with no experience at such things, failed to comprehend.

The coach had other unconventional features. In place of storm curtains the seats were protected by flats of sheet metal, heavy enough to stop an arrow and perhaps a bullet. The upper halves of the doors had been left clear for the sake of light and air—but mainly to give room for firing a rifle at attackers.

"Well," said Susan a trifle wanly, "at least we'll have a new racket to listen to as we bounce along from boulder to boulder. I imagine this tin stuffing will be quite noisy."

Even the front boot was armored as a refuge into which the driver could crouch. "An' here're some presents wid the best wishes of the Butterfield Overland Mail," Paddy O'Shay said. He placed Spencer rifles aboard. "In case of misfire ye each an' ivery one will be entitled to complain to the main office o' the company, God rest your souls. 'Tis ammunition ye will find in the boxes at your feet."

At least the load of mail had diminished. " 'Tis only patent-medicine pamphlets an' such trash that are in the sacks," O'Shay explained. "Valuable mail is not to be risked east of Tucson or west of El Paso 'til further orders, says the fideral gover'mint. I have orders to send first-class mail back to San Diego, where it will go by ship."

O'Shay turned, glaring around. "Cassman!" he bawled. "Alf Cassman!"

He went raging around, searching the station. He returned, sputtering. "The scut! There will be a delay. 'Tis the driver who's gone up a tree. He has run out on me."

"Afaid of Apaches?" Calhoun asked.

"I will find the craven creature," O'Shay vowed. "It might take a little time. He's taken to the brush, no doubt."

"It might take hours," Mike said. "I'll drive."

"It would not be regular," O'Shay said dubiously. "Not that I know ye can't do it, McLish. I know ye by reputation."

Fiske spoke. "If McLish is willing to volunteer, speaking

for myself, I'll be happy to have him take over. I have reason for haste."

Calhoun nodded agreement. "If we hang around here it means we'll hit the stretch through the mountains in daylight tomorrow. Our chances are better in the dark. I'm willing to risk it with McLish on the box. He probably values his neck as highly as I do mine."

O'Shay was still reluctant, but consented, obviously because it was Fiske's wish.

Mike mounted to the seat and called, "All aboard!"

"I'll ride on top, if you don't mind," Susan said.

Mike debated it a moment, then extended a hand and helped her to the seat beside him. There would be little danger for some distance out of Tucson. It would give them a chance to talk over their future course.

Mike appraised the team. They were horses. He had expected that mules would be used in the mountains, but these six animals were very adequate. The leaders were sinewy roans. The swings and wheelers were solid bays, and all the animals were obviously in top shape.

"Well, well!" Mike said. "Butterfield always did have the reputation of buying good livestock."

O'Shay had been awaiting his comment. He grinned, delighted. "Ye have the pick of all the livestock Butterfield owns between the Colorado River an' the Pecos," he said. "I gathered them meself. Sure an' a man wants good horseflesh in front of him through the Chiricahuas. So I told John Butterfield. He agreed. Not a horse there, but what can do the mile in under two-forty. See that ye treat my babies with proper respect."

Mike arranged the reins so that each finger had its duty and its horse to control. O'Shay gave a grunt of approval. "Ye have the know of it," he said.

"Hi-ya!" Mike called and kicked off the brake.

The horses snatched the mudwagon out of its tracks. Susan clung to the seat with one hand and held her scarf on her head with the other. She laughed excitedly. They were rolling at a fast clip, the horses working off their first burst of playfulness.

They followed a twisting road into broken country. The route dipped at times into arroyos and followed the courses of dry stream beds between clay walls.

Susan had quieted. Mike saw that she feared this country.

103

Spanish daggers stood with poised bayonets. Cholla, the fuzzy, villainous jumping cactus, crouched on the flanks of the hills. Occasionally the giant saguaro marched in ragged formation. Except for small lizards and kangaroo rats there was no sign of life in this savage land.

Mike gave her something else to think about. "You were right. Julia Fortune is carrying the stuff."

"Did she tell you so?"

"No. But I'm sure."

"She seemed to be confiding *something* to you in a rather intimate way."

"Were you spying?"

"Not intentionally. But I saw that you had your arm around her. Did you learn that she was stuffed with paper?"

Mike ignored that. "The fact that we know she's carrying it doesn't make it any easier. Tougher, maybe. We can't waste any more time."

"How do we go about it?"

"I know only one way. I'll put a gun on them if necessary. You'll have to search her. I'll see to it that Calhoun and Fiske don't interfere. Nor Lew Durkin."

"Lew Durkin?" She looked at him, startled.

Mike nodded. "Lew Durkin. The guerrilla. He's the one who calls himself Bill Jackson. Cass Bidwell recognized him at Fort Yuma. He and Calhoun are in cahoots. Calhoun probably rode with the Regulators back in Missouri."

Susan was quiet for a time. "All right," she finally said with the air of one taking an icy plunge. "When do we do it? This holdup?"

"At one of the stations, maybe," Mike said. "Or at any place the chance comes to catch them off guard."

"I—I haven't got a gun. Only those two hatpins."

"Are you still carrying those cursed things? If it was me I'd rather have you come at me with a gun."

Another silence came. "I couldn't use them on Julia," she said. "Nor a gun. I was wrong about her. She's decent. Decent in the things that count."

"Maybe you can bluff her."

"She isn't the kind who can be bluffed," Susan said. "You know that. But I'll try."

Susan sank back and resumed her weary gazing at rocks and cactus. When darkness came she returned to a seat inside the coach.

A driver to relieve Mike was on hand when they reached

Cienega Station after midnight. "But I ain't drivin' no further east than Dragoon," the man said positively. "I didn't sign up for no runs through 'Pache Pass. I ain't one danged bit sure that Cochise has pulled out. It's when you can't see 'em that your scalp is mighty loose on your head."

"Pike, here, is a no'therna," said the station agent, as though that explained everything. "No more spunk in him than a spring chicken."

"You know you'd be mighty glad to see even them blue-bellied cal'vry when they git here, Jem," the driver said.

"Maybe I'll see 'em over the bar'l of a rifle," the agent said. He was a Tennessean named Jem Cash.

Mike came to attention. "Did you say cavalry?" he asked the driver. "Federal troops. Where?"

"Didn't see 'em myself, but a driver who come through 'Pache Pass a few days ago said a company o' Union cal'vry was camped at Fort Fortymile. I reckon they're headin' for California to git out of secess territory."

"Fort Fortymile? Where's that?"

"Beyond 'Pache Pass Station a piece. Half a dozen miles, I reckon. Maybe more. The Army gave it some other fancy name when they built it, but everybody got to callin' it that because it's forty miles from nowhere."

"That must be at Rincon Spring," Mike said. "That's the only water east of the stage station."

"That's the place. You seem to have been in this country before. The Army laid out a fort there about two years ago to keep a thumb on Cochise an' his Chiricahuas. They built a rock stockade an' a few other buildings, but the post was abandoned before it was finished. That's the Army for you."

Mike was elated at the prospect of meeting troops on the dangerous route ahead. That faded as he noticed the way Fiske and Calhoun and Durkin were taking it.

Susan found a chance to speak to him alone. She too was happy. "We won't have to use a gun on them now," she whispered. "We can wait until we meet the soldiers and get help. They'll probably take them back to California under custody."

"Maybe," Mike said.

She eyed him. "You don't seem to be overjoyed."

"Something's wrong," Mike said. "It has the dull ring of a lead nickel."

"Why do you say that?"

"Our friends aren't as upset as they should be."

105

"Upset?" she demanded. "Why should they be?"

"Look," Mike said. "They could be facing charges of treason if they were caught by Union troops with incriminating papers on them."

"I see what you mean."

"This could be Fiske's own army," Mike said. "Anybody can wear a Federal uniform."

"Oh——" Her voice trailed off in dismay.

"But it could be Union troops, of course," Mike said. "There must be some still in the country. They couldn't all have pulled out by this time."

"Let's hope so," she said shakily.

"And now will you quit?" he demanded.

"Don't be foolish," she said. "I'm in no danger. They won't harm a woman. It's Julia Fortune we still have to deal with, remember. I'm sure you can't handle it alone."

"Why are you so sure?"

"She *is* very fascinating," she said.

She ended the talk by hurrying to take her place in the coach.

They arrived at Dragoon Springs shortly after noon. Cole Ringer, the stationmaster, was an Alabaman and made it very plain on which side he stood. He was obviously hostile to Mike. However, he knew Fiske and the two of them had a long and serious talk alone.

No relief driver was available. The man who had handled the reins from Cienega, true to his word, refused to go any farther.

Mike was back on the box as they pulled out of Dragoon, for Ringer had no other choice than to accept his offer. He at least had the advantage of a fair amount of sleep, for he had ridden inside the coach from Cienega.

Ahead now lay the Chiricahua Mountains, hunting grounds of Cochise's people. Ahead lay Apache Pass.

Susan again insisted on riding on top with him. He had consented, for the country was open for some distance out of Dragoon. The presence of cavalry in the mountains also seemed an assurance that the Apaches had pulled out.

When they were a few miles out from Dragoon, Mike, looking back, saw a lone rider following the trail, appearing and disappearing in the roll of the country. The horseman was too far away to be more than a dark speck and a small spurt of golden dust in the afternoon sun. Apparently he had passed through Dragoon not long after their departure. But his mount was not up to keeping pace with the stage and he fell farther astern.

After another hour Mike saw something else to the west. He kept glancing back whenever he could do so without attracting Susan's attention.

Finally she said quietly, "It's Dragoon Station burning, isn't it?"

The distant smoke was almost the same color as the gray-green land from which it arose. Dragoon was ten miles away now, and the smoke was visible only when the stage topped higher points.

"Somebody must have got careless with his pipe," Mike said. "Likely it's the haystack. They had a rick of wild hay back of the station. It was dry enough so that it would only take a spark of hot tobacco to set it going."

He knew she did not believe it.

Dragoon Station, where they had taken on fresh horses only a few hours ago, was on fire. The Apaches were back!

CHAPTER THIRTEEN

Mike let out the horses a notch. He tucked the whip beneath his arm, the long lash wrapped around the stock. The team understood. The coach began leaning on the thorough braces on the curves. The wheels slewed in sand. The six pairs of ears in the team were pinned back.

Fiske poked his head from the door below. "For God's sake, McLish! Are you crazy? You'll pile us up in a gully."

Mike pointed westward. Fiske gazed. After that there were no more questions. Reaching a barren stretch where it was unlikely that even an Apache could find concealment for an ambush, Mike halted the coach and let the horses catch their wind.

"You'll ride inside from now on," he said to Susan.

He drove on. He spared the team in the open stretches, but the whip popped when the trail would through brush and rocky defiles.

Fiske called out again. "McLish, we'd have an easier death at the hands of Apaches. Have mercy on us. We're being pounded to jelly."

Mike had no mercy on them. "Hang on, jellyfish!" he said.

The trail carried them into the Chiricahuas. The shadows deepened around them. The sun's glow climbed the peaks ahead and faded. Its last reflection left the flat-bottomed clouds and the stage moved through a growing purple twilight.

Mike pulled up on high ground where cooling air would reach them. The horses blew with vigor. They were working up lather, but were far from their limit. Paddy O'Shay's pride was justified. Butterfield stocked top horseflesh in the Apache country.

Calhoun alighted and helped rub the animals down. Durkin joined in the task. Mike realized that the horses were suddenly all standing with legs stiff and hoofs planted, sniffing the breeze uneasily. They were picking up some scent.

Mike moved clear of them. Then he caught it also. Smoke. And something else—acrid and terrifying. Burned flesh!

In the next moment this was gone from the night as the wind drew in another direction. Mike looked at the others. Apparently only he had detected the taint.

He mounted to the seat and drove the coach off the trail. Wheels crunched through stiff rabbit brush and lurched over small rocks. He halted in the shelter of brush big enough to hide the coach, for moonrise was near.

"What's wrong?" Calhoun asked.

"Trouble of some kind ahead," Mike said. "Something's on fire. I'm going to try for a look-see. Want to come?"

Calhoun accompanied him and they moved away through the darkness. After a time they had a wider view of the terrain.

A fire formed a sullen crimson pool in the blackness of a flat some distance ahead. A building was burning. Figures moved, outlined against the flames. They could make out the outline of a stagecoach. The coach also began to burn.

The breeze drew again in their direction and brought tortured screaming. Along with that arose a shrill yelping that might have come from animals. These were not animals.

They silently withdrew and returned to the coach. A sickness was in Mike.

He knew it would be a mistake to keep the truth from the others. "Apache Pass Station is gone," he said. "It's not far ahead—burning. They got a coach too. It must have been the westbound run. They probably waited until the coach pulled in, then hit the station. It would have been us if we'd got there first."

Fiske placed an arm around Julia. "Would it be better if we turned back?" he asked.

"It's probably as tough in that direction," Mike said. "With Dragoon gone we know there are at least two bunches of Apaches working the trail. There's probably more of 'em. Cochise didn't pull out. He only laid low for a few days to draw game into the trap."

They all turned, listening to the sound of hoofs on the trail. A shod horse. Mike remembered the rider he had sighted in the distance during the afternoon.

He walked nearer the trail and spoke guardedly. "You there! Pull up!"

The horse was halted. "Is that you, McLish?" a man asked.

"So help me!" Mike exclaimed. "I might have known!

Come off the trail before some Apache makes meat of you."

The arrival was Kirby Dean. He rode up and slid stiffly down from a weary horse. "I'm going to beat the tar out of you, McLish, as soon as I get the saddle kinks out of me," he said. "I've been trying for days to catch up with you to get hunk for slugging me back there on the desert."

"Now that'll be an interesting diversion," Mike said. "Do you take care of me first and the Apaches afterward?"

"So that's why you're skulking here off the road? They hit Dragoon not long after I traded for a fresh horse there. Have you seen any more sign of them?"

"They've wiped out Apache Station ahead," Mike said.

Susan came hurrying up. "You?" she exclaimed. "You— you—idiot!" She kissed him. She clung to him. She was torn between happiness at his presence and apprehension for him.

Mike led them back to the coach. Calhoun peered. "I'll be teetotally switched!" he exclaimed. "It's our friend with the yellow streak."

"That's right," Dean said. "You and I have some unfurnished business also, Calhoun."

"Name the time," Calhoun said.

"That will wait," Mike said. "The Apaches will likely take care of it for both of you anyway. But right now what we need is muscle instead of bravery."

"What's on your mind?" Lew Durkin asked.

"I'm familiar with this stretch of trail," Mike said. "The old San Antonio & San Diego Mail operated through the pass on this general route. That's the line they called the Jackass Mail because passengers often had to take to muleback when coaches weren't handy. I laid out a new road through this stretch when Butterfield took over. That's the one that's being used now. It lies higher on the mountain to avoid a lot of draws and grades the old trail followed."

"I see what you mean," Calhoun said.

"The old road is somewhere below us down the mountainside," Mike said. "It by-passes Apache Station. The old trail might still be passable. If we can reach it we might be able to sneak on through the pass before daybreak. The Apaches probably won't be expecting a stage to travel the old trail."

"It sounds reasonable," Calhoun said. "Fort Fortymile can't be far away."

"We'll have to wait for the moon to come up," Mike said. "We'll need all the light possible. Even then it'll be tough

110

enough to get this coach down the mountain in one piece."

"The coach?" Durkin objected. "Why bother with it? Why not ride the horses?"

"Some of these horses won't stand for being rode," Mike said. "They're harness-trained and would likely spill us all over the landscape. We're not in position to take care of any busted legs. The ladies would be better off in a coach."

"There's Dean's horse—" Durkin began.

"Nobody would get very far on him, I'm afraid," Dean said. "He's sulled. I was about to go it afoot when I bumped into you people."

Fiske spoke. "I say to abandon the coach."

"There are other reasons," Mike said. "In case we bump into trouble we'd have a chance of standing it off if we had the coach. It will make a pretty fair fort in a pinch."

"You can't get this thing down the mountain to this trail you say is there," Durkin raged.

"A big Concord, no," Mike said. "This mudwagon, perhaps. At least we've got better than an even chance."

"That's good enough for me," Kirby Dean said. "Let's get at it."

"I say to take the horses and get the hell out of here," Durkin snarled. "Damn the coach, and damn this thing of waiting for moonlight."

"We'll wait," Mike said. "And we'll keep the coach with us as long as possible."

They waited. Mike jettisoned the mail sacks. He debated doing the same with their baggage but finally decided to try to carry it with them.

The moon, past the full, silvered the crests of the ridges. With maddening deliberation it peeked down at them and slowly pulled clear of the skyline. Its light began probing the blackness of the canyons.

Mike, despite the smoldering impatience of Durkin and Calhoun, insisted on waiting until the mountainside was bathed in light. That delay wore on the nerves. Each time one of the horses moved a hoof or rattled a chain Mike heard the others around him quit breathing and listen. But these sounds were loud only on their own taut senses.

"All right," he finally said. He climbed to the driver's seat.

He hooked his feet in the boot loops so that he could not be easily dislodged from the coach in rough going and took an extra wrap in the reins.

111

He advised Fiske to stay near the coach, along with Susan and Julia. The others ranged ahead to signal the best route of descent.

Mike gazed at what he faced. The flank of the mountain dropped at a pitch that was steep, but not impossible. He could only hope that conditions were no worse beyond his line of vision. He would have to depend on the three men scouting ahead to warn him of any such danger.

"It might be only a little way to the old road," he said. "But it could be half a mile. I've no way of knowing."

He freed the brake and spoke to the horses. They rebelled at first, but his voice gave them confidence and they moved through the brush and onto the slant.

The wheels collided with a small, brush-hidden boulder. The horses tried to swing but Mike muscled them ahead and prevented that disaster. Once the wheels cramped, the coach would roll over and over down the slope. The vehicle climbed bodily over the boulder and landed upright with a crash.

"Swing to the right a little," Kirby Dean shouted. "You've got a sharper pitch ahead for a little piece. Hit it fast and straight downhill. It levels off just below so that you can slow down."

Mike complied. He let the horses run. It *was* steep. He was afraid the coach might tumble end-over-end upon the animals, but it remained upright and bounced unscathed onto a stretch of nearly level ground.

Mike halted the horses and took a deep breath.

"You'll get killed, McLish!" Fiske protested. "Give up. Let's abandon the coach."

Mike had to admire the man. He was sure that Fiske was aware that he, rather than the young women, was the reason Mike had insisted on trying to stay with the coach. Fiske was so near the end of his strength that he might have no chance of making it afoot.

"We might be almost there," Mike said. "One more little spurt and we could be out of the woods."

He urged the horses ahead and onto another descent. Calhoun stood ahead in the moonlight, waving arms, directing him to veer to the right.

Mike complied. He soon found himself on an increasing slant. He half-rose, peering. The descent seemed to end in the brush-fringed lip of a ledge.

Evidently Calhoun had overlooked the ledge. The drop was no more than a dozen or fifteen feet, perhaps, for beyond

112

the edge Mike could see more level mountainside, but that height was enough to shatter the coach and perhaps end his own life.

There was no stopping the coach. The brake-locked wheels slid ahead. And to attempt to veer off the direct line of descent would surely capsize the coach, sending it rolling over and over to the lip of the drop.

A heavier clump of scrub cedar grew just above the rim of the ledge and to the left. Mike grasped that chance. He veered the horses slightly in the direction of the cedar. He jerked the leaders sharply around a few jumps before they would have crashed into the foliage. The swings and wheelers followed, sliding and pawing for hoof-hold.

The coach slewed sideways and began to capsize. Mike tried to leap clear, but the swerve threw him off balance and he could not make it.

But his maneuver succeeded. The coach tilted on the off wheels as it crashed into the cedars. It ripped along, leaning crazily against the foliage until he could yank the horses to a sliding stop. It remained there, tilted among the cedar.

Kirby Dean came skidding down amid a small avalanche and helped quiet the horses. Calhoun and Lew Durkin arrived and gave a hand.

They unhooked the animals and led them clear. Mike alighted and said, "That was close."

With an ax from the jockey box they cut pry poles and succeeded in edging the coach onto open mountainside to the east of the ledge. A coil of rope was in the jockey box. Snubbing this around a cedar, they lowered the vehicle down the slant until it reached better going.

That used up more than an hour of muscle-straining labor. When it was over they all slumped down, exhausted. Mike soon aroused and examined the coach. The pole was cracked but he decided that it would still do the job. No other damage of any consequence had been done.

"You overlooked that ledge," he said to Calhoun.

"You misunderstood," Calhoun said. "I pointed to the right. You swung in the wrong direction."

Mike was sure Calhoun had deliberately tried to wreck the coach in order to get rid of it. He debated it, and Calhoun stood awaiting whatever move he might make.

Kirby Dean, realizing that bitter trouble was brewing, intervened. "We ought to get moving," he said.

Mike decided to let the matter ride. He explored down the

113

mountainside to make sure there would be no more mistakes, intentional or otherwise. Dean walked with him. In little more than two hundred yards they came upon the old trail.

They returned to the coach. Easing it the rest of the way down the slant offered no great problem. Soon it stood on the old trail which was now only a set of eroding wheel tracks, cut into the face of the mountain.

Mike scanned the slopes around them, and they stood listening, but there was no sign of danger. They resumed their places in the coach and Mike, with Dean beside him on the box, released the brake. They moved ahead.

There were short stretches where the horses could be stepped up to a trot but, for the most part, it was necessary to hold them down to a walk.

Often they all would alight and pitch in to build paths over washouts or slides, or to put their shoulders to the wheels and literally hoist the coach over fallen boulders or dead trees.

On two occasions they unloaded the baggage in order to lighten the vehicle. Mike was tempted to discard the luggage entirely, but decided against it mainly because he knew it would mean delay while the owners fished out any valuables they might insist on taking with them.

Dean spoke to Mike when they got under way after a stop that involved half an hour of sweating, frantic work, for they were now in a race against dawn.

"McLish," he said, "I've given up my intention of punching you on the jaw. For a man with scruples you still pull more than your share of the work. The fact is that I'm sort of beginning to take a liking to you."

"I'm happy to see you've abandoned that fake Dixie accent," Mike said. "A lot of things have changed since we left San Francisco. Was that weeks ago? Or years?"

"Centuries," Dean said.

"At least we know where the papers are," Mike said. "And the money. But that's all we do know."

"Damn the papers," Dean said. "Damn the money!"

Mike eyed him speculatively. Dean sounded sincere.

Again the leaders in the team slowed. Mike thrust a foot against the brake. "Another slide, folks," he said. "Everybody out. Ladies last."

Groaning, they alighted. Fiske insisted on helping, although Julia had been urging him to take it easy. He shed his coat and worked grimly. He strained at a wheel, helping to muscle the coach over a rockslide that blocked the route.

He stood back panting and pleased once the vehicle was past the obstruction. "It's been years since I felt the good ache of used muscle," he said. "It's grand hurt."

"It might be wiser if you took it a little easier," Mike advised. "You're not toughened to it."

Fiske started to tower, his pride stung. He swayed suddenly. Mike steadied him and Julia arrived. They helped him to the coach and he sank into a seat limply. "You were right, McLish," he said shakily. "I'm not as young as I thought."

Daybreak was near when they cleared the coach from the last tangle of brush and boulders. It lurched into the main trail and they drew deep, satisfying sighs. The road was clear and apparently vacant.

Mike drove eastward, wanting to put as much distance as possible between them and the purple ridges astern. After an hour they came into view of a long, open basin. Its flanks were clumped with the inevitable scrub cedar.

"Look!" Dean exclaimed.

A rock-built stockade stood in a flat ahead. Buildings showed inside the enclosure. A line of greenery marked a flowing spring just beyond the east walls of the place. Horses grazed there in the open, guarded by men in blue.

"Forty Fortymile," Mike said.

CHAPTER FOURTEEN

Fiske and Calhoun were peering from the window below. Mike looked down at them. Their expressions hardly fitted the situation. They might find themselves in deep trouble if these were Union soldiers at Fort Fortymile. The least they could expect would to be taken back to California in custody. They also stood a good chance of being summarily executed if war had actually broken out and the officer in charge of the detachment was excited. Yet they seemed undisturbed and even smiling a little, as though they were in on an amusing secret.

Mike urged the tired horses ahead. The appearance of the coach had brought activity at the fort. Men came hurrying through the open wagon gate to gaze.

Mike swung the coach past them into the enclosure and pulled up. The stockade walls, roughly built of rocks and adobe, were fitted with loopholes and firing embrasures. Buildings faced each other across a small parade ground where tumbleweeds had taken root. Two of these were of unpainted frame whose walls were weathering to the inevitable rust-brown hue of the desert. The smaller bore faded, painted signs proclaiming it as housing the post of the commanding officer and the orderly room. The other, larger and rambling, had been the sutler's store and supply shed.

Across the parade ground stood a sod-roofed, rock-built structure. The foundations of similar buildings had been started but never finished.

Men surrounded the coach. Mike's attention swung to them. The majority were dirty and unshaven. Their uniforms were disreputable.

Mike's gaze traveled from face to face. Here a flattened, broken nose, here an ear mangled in some brutal brawl in the past, here a face that must have come from some hellhole. One man, with swart features, wore gold earrings. Earrings on a man! Coarseness, grossness.

In the background stood half a dozen slatternly women

116

who were staring at Susan and Julia boldly and trading jeering remarks among themselves.

Mike looked at Kirby Dean. He also was staring in disbelief. Lew Durkin and Calhoun alighted. Fiske followed. Fiske still wore his air of satisfaction. This faded as his eyes moved around the circle. He seemed bewildered, shocked.

He turned to Calhoun. "These—these aren't our men?" he asked. The question was almost plaintive.

"Of course," Calhoun said. "What did you expect?"

Susan and Julia had started to alight from the coach, but they paused, staring in alarm at the garrison of Fort Forty-mile.

Mike spoke sharply. "What outfit do you men belong to?"

None answered. Their attention swung briefly to Mike, then returned to the two young women. They gazed impudently. Some of them laughed.

A man wearing the sword of an officer appeared from the post and came striding.

Lew Durkin spoke before anyone else could say a word. "I'm Bill Jackson. This is Vance Calhoun. These other people are passengers on this stage. 'Paches burned the station in the pass and Dragoon last night. We circled past them and got through."

The officer coughed and Mike believed that he wiped away a smirk. "Ah'm Lieutenant Booker," he said. "Ah'm in command here, temporarily of course, Mr. Jackson."

Mike decided that Booker was feeling his way and waiting for cues. He was a sharp-featured, unsavory individual with a grease-spotted tunic. He fitted right in with these caricatures of soldiers.

"We know there are formalities of course," Calhoun spoke. "Let's get them over with. We all need rest. Particularly the ladies."

He and Durkin were moving toward the post. Booker followed them. It was obvious that Durkin and Calhoun were giving the orders and that Booker was awaiting their lead.

Fiske moved to accompany them. Julia spoke. "Wait, Wheeler!"

Fiske halted and stood with his heavy shoulders drooping, staring with a stunned look at the door of the orderly room through which the three had vanished. Some of the ragtag soldiers laughed again.

A quarter of an hour passed. The sun cleared the horizon. Fiske did not move or look at Julia or at anyone. He merely stood there staring with that stricken blankness in his eyes at the closed door.

Mike and Dean rubbed down the horses, using wads of dry grass. None of the ragtag garrison offered to help. They merely crowded in closer.

Susan uttered a cry of indignation. Mike whirled. One of the men had reached into the coach and touched her hair.

Mike got to the offender a stride ahead of Dean. One of the uniformed men thrust a leg in Mike's path, intending to trip him. That was a mistake. He had underestimated Mike's size. Mike ran right through the leg with a force that spun its owner around. The man fell, groaning with a wrenched knee.

The one who had touched Susan tried to snatch out a sheath knife, but Mike was upon him. Mike's fist caught him at the base of the jaw, and he landed on his back near his moaning comrade. He lay there stunned.

Mike turned. Others of the scarecrow outfit were moving in.

Kirby Dean was at Mike's side, and he had pistols in his hands. " 'Tention!" he snapped.

The men slowed but began spreading to encircle them. Durkin and Calhoun came racing from the post. "Hold it!" Durkin bellowed. The men halted.

Durkin glared at Mike. "What the hell are you trying to do?"

Calhoun spoke. "We can go into that later. Let's not keep the ladies waiting any longer. Take us to these quarters you mentioned, please, Booker."

Booker motioned them all to follow him. Mike debated it, then decided there was no other course. He helped Susan and Julia from the coach.

Susan was pale. She eyed him questioningly. "We'll have to play it as it comes," he murmured.

He spoke to Booker. "What about the baggage?"

It was Calhoun who answered. "Some of the men will fetch it."

Fiske hesitated the longest. His face was putty-gray. The lost look persisted in his eyes. Julia took his arm and said gently, "It's best this way, Wheeler."

Booker led the way to the stone-built structure on the north side of the parade ground. It had two doors, only a few feet apart. The women were motioned to enter one of the

118

doors. Mike and the others were led through the second entrance.

Mike gazed around at a single long room. It had only two windows. These were very small. The room was separated from the opposite quarters by a wall of adobe and rock through which a low doorway opened. Two lengths of plank slung by leather straps from pegs in the wall served as a table. A bench and a bunk equipped only with a straw pallet and a ragged quilt completed the furnishings.

A rock-built fireplace occupied a rear corner of the center wall. It was sizable and evidently had served for both heating and cooking. The walls were liberally pierced with loopholes. Mike decided that the place had been intended as quarters for married officers, and had also been built with an eye to acting as a last stronghold in case of emergency. It stood well clear of the stockade walls.

Calhoun suddenly snatched Mike's pistol from his belt, cocked it, and jammed it against his chest. "Stand still!" he ordered.

Dean had been covered at the same moment by Durkin's drawn gun. Both were searched and disarmed. Mike's second pistol was taken, along with all the contents of his pockets.

Booker had searched and disarmed Fiske. "How blind can a man be?" Fiske said hoarsely to Calhoun.

Durkin opened Mike's wallet which contained the cash and the drafts Alexander Majors had given him. Calhoun curtly waved aside his share. Durkin laughed and divided the money between himself and Booker. He pocketed the drafts, saying, "Maybe I can do something with these too."

"We'll be back later," Durkin said. He and his companions moved outside where Durkin shouted orders. Presently men came with spikes and wagon chains with which they secured the door that connected the two rooms.

Both outer doors were chained shut also. Planks torn from the sutler's shed were spiked across the small windows, leaving only crevices for light.

After a time the majority of the guerrillas had wandered back to their camp. Mike tested the door, thrusting his weight against it. The chains clanked but the portal barely quivered.

A voice spoke. "Stay away from that door, you. I got orders to put a bullet in anybody thet gits gay in there."

119

"Scum!" Fiske raged. "Riffraff! So these are the kind of men the Union has for soldiers!"

"They're not soldiers and you know it," Mike said. "You might as well quit trying to fool yourself, Fiske. They're your own men."

Fiske moved exhaustedly to the bunk and sank down. "No, McLish," he said. "Not these brutes."

"What do you really know about Calhoun?" Mike asked.

"I took him at face value," Fiske admitted. "I've realized only lately how badly mistaken I was. I trusted him. What do you know about him?"

"I know that he's hand-in-glove with this man who calls himself Bill Jackson and that Bill Jackson's real name is Lew Durkin. You've heard of Durkin, the Regulator, haven't you?"

Horror grew in Fiske. "Are you sure? Then these men are—are——"

"Guerrillas," Mike said. "Cutthroats. Durkin's Regulators are back in business. Calhoun is one of them."

"God help me!" Fiske breathed. "I'm responsible."

"You are," Mike said. "You know what men like this can do, don't you? They don't give a hoot about the Union or the Confederacy. If they get to San Francisco they'll loot it and probably burn it down. That's the way of their kind. How many of them are there in all?"

"Calhoun told me that Jackson—Durkin—had recruited more than two hundred."

"There can't be more than fifty here."

"This is only the advance guard," Fiske said. "The others are still at El Paso, I suppose."

"I doubt that," Mike said. "He probably lied to you. This is the whole outfit. They probably figured on picking up more men at Los Angeles and along the way. But I understand you were financing a second bunch that was to come by way of Panama. Did Durkin and Calhoun organize that part of it too?"

"Yes," Fiske said. "But they were still waiting for money to pay for the ship charter at Galveston Bay."

"If this outfit we're up against doesn't make it, the whole thing is washed up," Mike said. "That's the size of it, isn't it?"

Fiske nodded numbly. "You seem to know all about me," he said. "Roger Vickers, of course. He is always very thorough."

"So it's no surprise to you that I know Vickers?"

"No," Fiske said. "I was certain almost from the start

that Vickers had sent Miss Lang and Mr. Dean. You were the one I wondered about. That trap we set at Vallecito was meant for you. You didn't fall into it, but it proved that you were working with them. Roger Vickers is a very capable opponent. I have great respect for him."

Dean spoke harshly. "Respect enough to try to have him murdered."

"I had nothing to do with that," Fiske protested. "I knew nothing about it until I read the account in Los Angeles."

"Why would you stop at murder?" Dean demanded. "You don't have any qualms about risking Julia Fortune's life in this business. This thing you're doing is treason."

Fiske was suddenly grim and hostile. "I would use anyone or anything to help the secession. Even Julia, and she's the only person in the world I'd lay down my own life for."

Dean started a bitter answer, but Mike motioned him that it was useless and he subsided.

Mike walked to the fireplace. No blaze had been built there for months. He peered up the blackened throat of the flue. It was set at the usual angle and he could see the glow of daylight from above down the main chimney.

He spoke guardedly. "Susan? Can you hear me?"

He heard the swish of skirts. Susan's voice sounded close at hand in the chimney. "Yes. I hear you."

"These two fireplaces come together just above and use the same chimney to the top," he said. "Are you all right?"

"Yes, but locked in. Who are these men? They frighten me."

"It'll work out," Mike said. "Sit tight."

Fiske came to Mike's side. "Julia!" he spoke.

Julia answered. "Yes, Wheeler."

Fiske spoke in a tense whisper. "Destroy it, Julia. Get rid of it. Burn it. I have matches. I believe I can toss the block to you. There seems to be a double throat to this chimney. Burn it all. At once. The money, above all. That's what they're really after."

"I would if I still had it," she said. "But I haven't."

"What? What became of it?"

"I hid it last night."

"Where?" Fiske demanded.

She didn't answer immediately. "I decided to hide it while we were struggling over the old stage trail," she said.

"I see. You hid it somewhere along the trail. But where?"

Again she delayed before answering. "I believe it's better that you don't know, Wheeler."

Fiske understood. He gave an impatient snort. "These scoundrels can't force me to tell anything I don't care to tell," he said. "But you—"

"I'll never tell them either," she said.

Kirby Dean spoke sharply. "That's being foolish, Julia. You don't understand. These men will play rough."

"I understand perfectly," Julia said. "Wheeler thought he was leading a crusade. Instead, these men are thugs and butchers."

"Then you know what'll happen if you try to buck them," Dean said. "Nothing's worth that."

"I've suspected for some time what kind of a man Calhoun is," Julia said. "He knows those men would never let us go even if they did get the money."

Fiske desperately tried to debate it. Mike finally halted him. "It's no use," he murmured. "She's made up her mind. They might be listening. You're talking too loud."

They all quit talking. Mike peered through a slit between the planks at a window which overlooked the parade ground. Their weathered mudwagon had been placed beside two canvas-topped supply wagons which stood between the sutler's building and the command post. The horses had been led away.

The boot stood open and empty, the straps dragging. Their baggage had been carried inside the post to be searched, and there was little chance they would ever see it again, Mike realized.

He again moved to the fireplace and spoke. "Susan?"

She answered at once. She must have been near, waiting. Now that he had started it he couldn't find the right words. "I'll give a plenty if we can ever get you out of this," he blurted out.

Her voice was warm. "Mike McLish," she said. "That's the first time you've said anything to me that I liked to hear."

"I'd like a chance to say a few others things," Mike said.

"Keep talking," she said. "It helps. I'm shaking. Mike, I'm scared."

"You've nothing to worry about," Mike said. "They're stalled as long as they can't get their hands on the money. They'll finally give it up as a bad job."

Neither of them belived that, but it sounded optimistic at least.

"Mike," she said. "No matter what happens they won't touch either Julia or me. We've agreed on that."

122

Her voice went on without emphasis or emotion. "I've kept the hatpins. Julia and I each have one. They really aren't hatpins. They're much stronger. They were made especially to be used as weapons in case of trouble."

Fiske had not heard that, for he was stretched on the bunk, exhausted. But Dean was near. He moved closer and spoke. "Sue! Julia!"

Mike turned and walked away. Whatever they had to say, he decided, was not supposed to be for his ears. At least it was nothing he wanted to hear. The emptiness, which had vanished while he had talked to Susan, now returned.

CHAPTER FIFTEEN

Presently Mike heard footsteps approach. The door was opened to admit Durkin and Calhoun. Durkin had a cocked pistol in his hand, but Calhoun had not bothered to draw either of his brace of weapons.

Booker's face appeared at their shoulders, but Calhoun closed the door on him, shutting him out.

"Stand where you are, all three of you," Durkin said. "Don't come any closer or I'll kill you."

He turned his attention to Fiske. "We want the bonds and the money," he said. "Where are they?"

Fiske had left the bunk and was on his feet, haggard and unsteady. "They're in a place you'll never find," he said.

"Do you know who I am?"

"Yes. You're Lew Durkin. But I only became aware of it lately. Vance, you were too clever for me. You fooled me completely. I had come to look on you almost as a son. I could not have been more sadly mistaken."

"You were asked a question, Wheeler," Calhoun said. "Where's the money?"

Fiske shook his head. "It's no use, Vance. You'll never get your hands on it."

"We've searched the coach and the baggage," Calhoun said. "It wasn't there. So it's either on you or that harlot."

Fiske took a stride toward Calhoun. "Harlot?" he rasped. "That's a lie. You try to defile her because you know she loathes you."

Kirby Dean stepped in ahead of Fiske. "I'll take care of this," he said.

Durkin's pistol veered on Dean. He would have shot him down, but Mike shoved both Dean and Fiske back. "Fiske's telling the truth," he said. "There's no money here. It's far away."

"What do you mean—far away?" Durkin asked grimly.

124

Fiske answered before Mike could speak. "I hid it back along the trail in the mountains last night."

Dark, angry blood came into Durkin's heavy features. Mike saw a vein at Calhoun's temple begin to throb. It came to him that the money Fiske had carried probably was the bait that had held their guerrilla outfit together this far.

"Quit stalling!" Durkin warned. "Why would you hide it back in the mountains?"

"Partly because we stood a good chance of being caught by the Apaches at that time," Fiske said. "But mainly because I had started to suspect Calhoun here. I had finally begun to listen to Julia. She told me at Fort Yuma that she believed you were up to some sort of treachery, Vance."

"You're lying," Calhoun snapped. "The money is on Julia, isn't it? She's carrying it in her clothing."

Durkin spoke. "He needs a little prodding to make him talk, Vance. Jolt him a little."

Calhoun drew one of his pistols, cocked it, and fired. Fiske staggered, groaning, his left arm shattered by the bullet. Blood spurted.

It was the callous casualness of the act that horrified Mike above all. He heard Julia scream. He moved toward Fiske to help him.

"Stay away from him, McLish!" Durkin warned. "And you too, Dean, or we'll clip a wing for you too."

Fiske steadied himself and pushed Mike aside. "I'll never tell you where it is, Vance," he said. "And you'll never find it."

Mike believed Calhoun would have fired a finishing shot into Fiske except that he realized he might be silencing the only person who knew the location of the money. Calhoun and Durkin looked at each other. They were stalled for the moment, and they knew it.

Durkin glared at Mike. "Tie up Fiske's arm," he growled. "See to it that he doesn't bleed to death. I'll hold you responsible."

He and Calhoun tramped out. The door was chained in place again. Mike and Dean helped Fiske to the bunk. They slit away his shirt and examined the wound. The bullet had evidently shattered the bone above the elbow but had passed on through. It was an ugly injury. They bandaged it as best they could and succeeded in checking the loss of blood.

When Mike removed the tourniquet Fiske slumped back into a coma. Mike believed for a time that he was never coming out of it, but he rallied at last, although he lay ash-gray and in a daze of pain.

Mike and Dean suddenly straightened, listening. Durkin's voice was audible in the adjoining quarters. "Howdy, ladies!"

Susan answered. "What do you want?"

"From you, maybe nothing," Durkin said. "But this other gal might be of help to us."

His voice roughened. "You know what we want. Where is it? The money?"

Julia answered. "It's hidden, just as we told you. But Mr. Fiske doesn't know where it is. I was the one who hid it. I'm the only one who knows. He only said that so as to take the responsibility."

"It's hidden on you right now," Durkin said. "It's being carried in your clothes. Isn't that right?"

"It was until last night," Julia said. "I've carried it ever since we left Los Angeles. I sewed it into the lining of a petticoat. But I hid the petticoat last night where you'll never find it."

Calhoun spoke. "It's no use, Julia. We don't believe you."

"We'll damned soon find out," Durkin said. "Get your clothes off!"

Julia started a protest, but he broke into a rage. "Be quick about it, or I'll rip them off you!" he exploded.

"I'll take them off," Julia said, and her voice was still steady, "but only after you two leave the room. I'll hand them out to you through the door."

Durkin laughed. "Now don't try to act shy and modest, lady. We know better. We're staying right here and——"

His voice trailed off. There was a moment of silence. Durkin spoke again. "What's that you've got there?"

"It looks like a hatpin," Julia said. "But it is really a very vicious little rapier."

"You don't think I'm afraid of a damned hatpin or whatever it is, do you?" Durkin said.

"I don't intend to use it on you," Julia said. "Although that would be a pleasure. I'll use it on myself if necessary. That will be when you come one more step toward me."

Silence came again. Mike saw that Kirby Dean's face was ashen, and he knew that his own must be the same hue. There was no misunderstanding. Julia meant exactly what she said.

Calhoun broke the silence. "Julia! You wouldn't do a thing like that!"

Susan spoke for the first time. "You know she will. And I've got a hatpin too. None of you will ever touch either of us. Make up your minds to that."

Durkin broke into profanity. Calhoun, with his icy way of accepting a situation, compromised. "If we send in two women, will you hand your clothes over to them for us to search?"

"If they are given back to us afterwards," Julia said.

"Of course," Calhoun said.

He added, "That includes you also, Miss Lang."

"Me?" Susan exclaimed.

"You! For all we know, the money could have been passed to you. We intend to make sure, and I'm nearing the end of my patience. And another thing—there'll be no point in trying to hide it in this room. The place will be searched."

"These women are not to touch us," Susan said.

"Agreed," Calhoun said.

Durkin stepped outside and shouted orders. Two of the slatternly camp followers presently arrived. Mike heard their shrill voices in the adjoining room.

From the sounds, the agreement apparently was being kept. Presently the other women left and Mike heard the outer door being closed and chained.

Durkin's guerrillas had gathered outside. Ribald comment arose. "Purty, ain't they?" one guffawed. "What do you call them things, Lew?"

"Look at them lace gadgets," another howled. "Now there's somethin' that needs fillin' to be appreciated."

"One thing's fer danged sure, Lew," another yelled. "It ain't hid in them things Mag's holdin' up. You kin see right through 'em."

"Just what are you lookin' fer, Lew?" another asked. "Maybe you're only tryin' to find out the latest styles right down to bare facts."

The badinage faded out of hearing as the guerrillas followed Durkin and Calhoun across the parade ground where the two entered the orderly room, carrying the garments.

Fiske was conscious and had been listening. "Try to persuade Julia to lead them to the cursed money," he said faintly.

"Her only protection is that they don't know where it is," Mike said. "That's all that's keeping any of us alive."

"My fault!" Fiske gasped. "All my fault."

Susan's voice sounded guarded. "Come to the fireplace, Mike."

Mike complied. "Lucky the weather has turned warm today," he commented.

"This is not the time for your low type of humor," she said. She dropped her voice to so low a pitch he had to strain to hear her. "Do you know something? I think I can squeeze my way up this chimney and reach the roof."

"Now don't get any loco ideas," Mike said quickly. He twisted, gazing up into the throat of the fireplace. "It can't be done anyway. It's not big enough even for a child."

"I'm sure I can get through, but I might need a little help. I'm not exactly plump, you know."

"So I've noticed. And what would you do, even if you got up there?"

"Maybe I could figure a way to get all of us out of here," she said.

"And fall into more trouble than you can take care of," Mike said.

"You ought to be able to squeeze a little way into the fireplace on your side," she said. "If I could make it to the top of this dividing wall maybe you could give me a lift. But don't experiment now. If they saw any soot on either of us they'd guess what was up. We'll wait until dark."

Mike couldn't debate it, for the guerrillas were returning. Julia spoke hurriedly. "Wheeler?"

Fiske answered. "Yes, Julia."

"Are you hurt?"

Fiske found the strength to speak lightly. "It's only a scratch. They merely creased me, trying to frighten me."

She had to be satisfied with that. The door of the women's quarters was flung open.

"There's yer blasted clothes!" one of the camp followers shrilled. "Get dressed, an' hurry up about it. The captain's comin' to search this here room."

Presently Mike could hear Calhoun and Durkin in the room, ransacking. Evidently the search was futile, for the pair came to the room where Mike and his companions were held. They had pistols in their hands.

Calhoun's icy calm had broken. Along with Durkin, he was in a livid rage. He walked to the bunk and jammed

128

the bore of a gun against Fiske's head. "Tell that vixen she'll be wise if she leads us to the stuff and in a hurry!" he said. "Or I'll scatter your brains over this room."

Mike spoke. "And if she does?"

Lew Durkin whirled on him. "What've you got to say about it?"

"I'll do the talking from now on," Mike said. "For all of us."

"The hell you will! Then talk! And fast!"

"She'll show you where the money is on one condition," Mike said.

"We set the conditions, not you!" Calhoun snapped.

"We set them," Mike said. "You've got a bear by the tail and you know it."

"You might be too cute for your own health," Durkin said.

"Cute enough to know that this outfit won't hold together forever unless there's some hard cash in sight—and soon," Mike said. "You need that money to keep them interested. And you likely need it to sweeten the pot for the outfit that's supposed to move in on San Francisco by way of Panama."

He saw that Durkin was on the point of shooting him down. "The conditions is that the women go free," he said.

"Of course," Calhoun said quickly.

"You're a little too quick on the draw when it comes to promises," Mike said. "Particularly when you've got no choice. First, let's make sure you'll keep your word."

"What've you got in mind?" Durkin demanded. He had lowered the pistol a trifle.

Mike could feel his pulse hammering. He had been on the edge of death and had stepped back. "It's too late to do anything today," he said. "It'll be dark in an hour. We'll talk it over in the morning. Another condition is that we be given decent food and bedding. And medical help for Fiske."

"Refused!" Calhoun said. "Starve and shiver. You're right about only one thing. It's too late to do anything more today. We'll be back by morning. I advise you to be more humble by that time."

He and Durkin walked out and the door was chained.

Mike listened to their receding footsteps. He and Dean traded glances. All that he had done was to delay the issue. He had no plan. He had only succeeded in stalling for time.

"Mike!" Susan called. "Come here and listen to me!"

Mike reluctantly returned to the fireplace. Dean listened in also.

129

"What is it?" Mike asked.

"Now stop that!" she said impatiently. "You know very well what I want to talk about. The chimney."

"It's too dangerous, of course," Mike said. "Otherwise I'd try it myself."

"You? You'd stick in it like a cork in a bottle and you know it. As for being dangerous, just what do you call it, staying in this room, waiting for those men to come in?"

"Even if you got on the roof what could you do except get yourself shot?" he demanded.

"There's been only one man on guard all day," she said. "Maybe that's all they'll have there tonight. I've worked a rock loose from the fireplace. I can make a sling of it in a stocking. If I can sneak up on him, I'll use it. Then I can turn all of you loose. We might be able to get away."

Dean spoke sharply. "Sue!"

She answered reluctantly. "Now don't try to lecture me, Dean. My mind's made up."

"Don't try it!" Dean implored. "Listen to me! Don't you dare try it!"

Mike spoke apprehensively. "Of course she won't."

"Do you hear me, Sue?" Dean insisted. "Answer me! Confound it! Don't try it!"

Mike grew panicky. "She wouldn't, would she?" he asked.

"Of course she would," Dean said. "You don't know her."

"And you do?" Mike snapped.

"Yes. I know her very well. I told you once before that she was mule-stubborn."

"But she will listen to reason?" Mike said desperately.

"She never has yet. She does the damnedest things. How do you suppose she got mixed up in this business in the first place? She insisted on it."

"Pay no attention to him," Susan whispered. "I'll wait until along toward the middle of the night."

"I'll have nothing to do with this foolishness," Mike said. "Do you hear me?"

"If you could get through that chimney you'd try it in a second," she sniffed. "You be there to help me when I give the word, Mike McLish, or I'll never speak to you again."

Mike and Dean were silent for a time. Dean asked, "Do you still have the hatpin, Sue?"

A tremor came in her voice. "Yes. I'll take it with me, along with the rock."

After that nobody could think of anything more to say. Dusk deepened in the room. Darkness came. The guerrillas kept their word. No food was brought, nor bedding. With the sun gone, a chill came in the room. Mike knew that at this season the temperature might drop to freezing before morning.

The moon, past the full, came up, its glow bright around the crevices in the windows. The guerrilla camp was noisy for some time. Evidently a liquor ration had been passed out. On one occasion drunken men came pounding at the door of the adjoining room. They left only when Calhoun arrived and threatened to shoot them.

"You ought to be grateful for my protection, Julia," Calhoun called.

Julia did not answer and he went away. Fiske spoke hoarsely.

"McLish! Call Calhoun back. Tell him I'll lead him to the money. But only if the rest of you—every one of you—are released."

"He wouldn't keep his word," Mike said. "You know that. As long as he hasn't got his hands on the money we've all got a chance of staying alive."

"He'll force Julia to tell," Fiske said. "These people won't stop at torture."

Mike had no answer for that. Fiske spoke again. "My plan would buy time for us. A day might be enough."

"Enough for what?"

"Some of your Butterfield men should be within a day or two's march of us," Fiske said. "They've got an escort of Union cavalry. A full company."

Mike and Dean moved quickly nearer the bunk. "What's that you're saying?" Mike demanded.

"The order to abandon Butterfield has come through," Fiske said. "All the stations east of here as far as the Pecos have been deserted. A column of coaches and stock is heading this way, trying to make it to California ahead of whatever pursuit there might be by Texas troops. The majority of your damned Butterfield crews turned out to be Unionists. The whole pack and rabble of them are being guarded by cavalry."

"How do you know this?"

"The stationmaster at Dragoon Springs," Fiske said. "Cole Ringer. A dispatch rider had come through only a few hours before we reached Dragoon. He brought word. Ringer, being an Alabama boy, was fixing to grab all the stock and equipment at Dragoon and head for Texas. But the Apaches must have got there first."

"Most likely it was this bunch of guerrillas in Union uniforms that Ringer was talking about," Mike said.

"No," Fiske said. "He knew about these men here at Fort Fortymile. I knew about them too. Calhoun, of course, had told me that he had received word from Bill Jackson, as Durkin called himself, that this place was to be the assembling point. How gullible I was! I didn't realize how completely he had played me for a fool until I stepped out of the coach inside this stockade."

"Does Calhoun know?" Mike asked.

"That a Union force is in the country? No. I asked Ringer to keep it between the two of us. I was already uneasy about Calhoun even though I didn't realize how completely wrong I had been about him."

Dean spoke. "You said you thought this Butterfield column was only a day or two away. How do you know that?"

"It's only an estimate," Fiske said. "Ringer's information was a week old when he talked to me. At that time they had been moving west from Mesilla. If they've kept traveling they should be within forty or fifty miles. They can't move too fast because they're driving loose stock with them and there are some women and children along. Families of station men."

Mike estimated distances and shrugged. "There's no telling. They might be showing up at any minute, or it might be two or three days. And if they're being chased by secess troops they might never show up at all."

"That's why my idea is best," Fiske said. "It'll win at least a day's time. Maybe longer."

"If one of us could slip out of here and get in touch with them, the troops could come up on the double," Dean said.

He and Mike, impelled by the same thought, moved to the fireplace and peered up the chimney. They could see moonlight reflecting faintly down the opening.

Mike backed out of the fireplace. "I couldn't make it," he said. "It's suicide."

Dean tested the opening. He was more slender, but he also was defeated. "It can't be done!" he gasped, fanning away soot.

Susan spoke from the opposite side. "I can make it."

"No," Mike said. "We've got another idea."

"Bah!" she said. "I've heard you whispering. Mr. Fiske

132

wants to lead them on some sort of a wild-goose chase. That'll only make things worse."

"Do you really think you can get through that chimney?" Dean asked.

"I can at least try."

"Fiske tells us there's help somewhere east of us if we can get in touch with it," Dean said. "Butterfield has abandoned. Men and coaches are heading this way. They've got an escort of troops with them. That makes the situation a little different."

Hope flared in her voice. "Now I *know* I can squeeze through that thing."

"And get yourself killed!" Mike rasped. He turned on Dean. "You don't give a damn what happens to her, do you?"

"You don't know how wrong you are!" Dean snapped.

The sentry outside lifted his voice. "What's all that mumblin' about in there? Maybe you all want to be tied up an' gagged. Quiet down now an' go to sleep."

They quit talking and waited. An hour passed by. The guard was changed. This duty evidently was limited to three-hour spells.

The guerrilla camp had quieted. Mike could hear the new sentry moving around occasionally, his boots scuffing the coarse soil. The coarse tang of cheap tobacco smoke drifted into the room. The night brought other sounds, the twittering of birds in the brush as some foe prowled for food, the grunting of an owl. Mike became aware of the drowsy activity of the guerrillas' horses on the stable lines.

After a long time a new sound became evident. The guard was snoring.

Susan's whisper came. "That scoundrel out there is asleep. I'm going to try it."

"Don't be afraid to change your mind," Mike said.

"I'll get cold feet if I put it off a minute longer," she chattered. "They'll change guard before long. A new one will be wide awake. I'm starting. I've got the hatpin and the rock."

Mike heard her wriggle her way into the opposite throat of the chimney. Dean crowded into the fireplace, peering anxiously upward. Mike pushed him aside. "I've got a longer reach than you," he said.

Susan gasped, "Give me a hand if you can reach me!"

Mike jammed his head and shoulders partly into the black maw of the opening. It was no smooth passageway. Its face

133

was armored with the sharp corners of sledge-broken rock.

His outstretched hand reached the top of the dividing wall. His fingers closed on a knee which was covered only by a thin silk garment.

"Lift!" Susan panted, pushing her way higher. "Lift me!"

Mike braced himself and hoisted. A cloud of soot descended on him. The knee was withdrawn. In its place came a bare foot, which she planted firmly in his palm.

She had succeeded in wriggling to a full-length position in the main chimney, and he was supporting her entire weight on his one hand.

"Just a little higher!" she implored. "Just a few inches. I can almost reach the top."

Mike strained upward, jamming his shoulders deeper into the opening.

Suddenly the weight was gone from his extended hand. More soot rained down. He saw moonlight again through the fog of soot. The chimney above him was clear! She had made it. She was on the roof.

With Dean dragging at his legs Mike extricated himself from the chimney. He lay with his head wrapped in his arms, smothering the sneezing and snuffling until he could breathe normally.

CHAPTER SIXTEEN

Mike and Dean strained to listen. Faint creaking came from the heavy beams that supported the sod roof. Particles sifted down, their rattle agonizingly loud.

A muted thud followed. The creaking ended overhead. Susan had reached the ground at the rear of the building.

There was no further sound for so long that Mike found his throat leather-dry. He wanted to speak, to move. But he remained utterly motionless and silent.

He heard Dean swallowing hard. Fiske and Julia made no sound. All of them were waiting, trying to listen.

Sound, when it came, was very emphatic. It was as though someone had struck a wooden post with the flat of the hand. A weight fell against the door. That was followed by a bubbling and groaning. They heard a body being dragged aside.

The chains were being removed from the doors. The door swung free.

"Help me!" Susan whispered frantically.

The guard was huddled against the wall alongside the door. His rifle lay alongside him and also the stocking-slung stone that Susan had used on him.

Mike looked at her. Suddenly he took her in his arms and kissed her. She responded emphatically. "McLish, I'm covering you with soot," she babbled hysterically.

"Beautiful soot!" Mike said. "But you're a little late. I'm already covered."

"I've turned into a chimney sweep," she said.

"A wonderful occupation," Mike said. "It becomes you."

Dean spoke angrily. "This is a hell of a time for holding hands!" He was kneeling beside the crumpled guard.

"Is—is he dead?" Susan chattered. "I tried not to hit him too hard. He woke up and jumped to his feet just as I got close to him."

The sentry was not dead. He was, in fact, showing signs of reviving. He had been carrying an Enfield rifle and a

135

holstered navy cap-and-ball pistol. A bayonet hung in a belt scabbard. He was partially uniformed in a cavalry tunic and hat. Mike stripped these from him and donned them. He and Dean tied and gagged the man, using his belt and shirt for the purpose. They dragged him inside the building.

Fiske joined them, unsteady on his feet. Julia, seeing the bandage, rushed to him. "You *are* hurt!" she breathed.

"I never felt better in my life," Fiske blustered.

He turned to Susan and kissed her on the cheek. "Thank you, my dear," he said. "You are very brave."

Mike silenced them. "We'll talk later. First, we've got to get out of here."

"We'll grab horses," Dean said. "The main bunch is outside, but there are some over there inside the wall."

Mike debated it, trying to decide whether Fiske was strong enough to ride. But it at least offered him a chance for living. He had none here. And, for the sake of Julia and Susan, it had to be tried.

The guerrilla bivouac remained silent. Light showed in the orderly room across the parade ground. Someone evidently was on duty there. No doubt there would be men guarding the horses.

About a dozen animals were held inside the stockade, as best Mike could make out in the moonlight. Evidently this was a precaution so that mounts would be available in an emergency.

He handed the guard's rifle to Fiske. "Dean and myself will try to cut out horses to ride," he said. "We'll stampede the rest. You stay with the ladies. All of you be ready to ride hell for leather."

He added, "If this doesn't work out, the three of you barricade yourself in the house and talk terms with them."

He handed the bayonet to Dean and kept the pistol. Susan halted Dean and kissed him. She clung to him, talking to him, and dabbing at her eyes.

Mike turned away. He was thinking that the way she had responded to his own kiss hadn't meant what he had believed it had. He felt unutterably weary.

Dean turned from Susan and took Julia Fortune in his arms. He kissed her also, and with deep tenderness. She too began to weep. He released her and joined Mike. "All right," he said.

Mike only said, "Later."

"Be careful, McLish!" Susan said fiercely.

"The way you were careful?" he snorted. "Running around in the moonlight almost naked and slugging a man with a rock?"

He kept going. He wanted no more sentimental scenes with her. He might say or do something foolish. Something all of them would regret. He might tell her how sorry a spectacle she was making of herself, pretending to be blind to the way Julia Fortune had taken Dean's affections from her. And using him, Mike McLish, as a sop to her pride.

"Stay well back of me," he said. "I'm going to walk up to the horses, bold as brass, pretending I'm one of the guerrillas. There's bound to be someone on guard, but the hat might fool them long enough for me to get close."

Holding the pistol concealed, he walked to the rear wall of the stockade. It was pierced by a wagon gate built of two wings. One wing stood open. Mike passed through it and moved toward the dark mass of horses. They were tethered, army style, on stable lines.

A voice spoke near-at-hand. "Who's thet?"

"Just me," Mike said. "Is that you, Bill?"

He located his man. The guard stood in the shadow of the stockade wall just out of reach of the moonlight. Mike kept walking and got within arm's reach before the man became suspicious and straightened from his lax slouch.

Mike struck with the muzzle of the pistol. But the luck that had been running their way left him. The guard instinctively parried the blow with his rifle. He tried to veer the rifle around to fire into Mike's body.

Mike, off balance, managed to bat the muzzle away a moment before it exploded. The bullet went wide. Mike swung the pistol in a savage backlash. This time it connected solidly on the man's temple, felling him.

The explosion of the rifle had crashed against the walls of the stockade and the deep echoes were still rolling in the hills. The startled horses began rearing on their tethers.

Dean came rushing up. "Are you hit?" he demanded.

"No, but the fat's in the fire!" Mike said. "There's no chance now of all of us getting away. You'll have to try it alone."

The sentry's saddled horse stood picketed nearby, having been kept handy in case of need.

Mike took the bayonet from Dean's hand and slashed the picket line. "Up you go!" he said. "Ride!"

Dean resisted Mike's attempt to push him toward the horse. "Why not you?" he protested.

137

"Dammit!" Mike said frantically. "You're lighter than me. It's our only chance now. Try to find these Feds. The rest of us can fort up in the house and hang on until you get back. You're the one that's taking the big chance."

Dean still hesitated, but Mike lifted him almost bodily into the saddle and thrust the reins in his hand.

"No telling how good this horse is," Mike panted. "Favor him and save something in case you hit trouble. Watch out for Apaches when it comes daylight. Take the pistol. You might need it. We'll still have the rifle, and I might be able to round up some more. I'll stampede the rest of these horses so they can't chase you."

Dean leaned from the saddle and gave him a mighty whack on the back. "McLish," he said as he kicked the horse into motion, "I'd be a mighty sad man if we never met again."

Then he was on his way at a gallop. Mike ran down the line, slashing picket ropes with the bayonet. He lifted a screeching war whoop. That touched off a total stampede. He darted inside the stockade and freed the horses there. These poured through the gate and joined the flight. The animals thundered away into the moonlight, heading for the ridges.

The guerrillas were swarming from their bivouac at the west end of the enclosure.

"Paches!" Mike yelled. "They're stealin' the stock!"

He scuttled in shadow along the east wall of the stockade and then followed the south wall until he was at the rear of the two frame buildings. He crouched there.

His shout had been taken up and repeated. The guerrillas were running across the parade ground and through the rear gate in the wake of the departing horses. All were carrying guns they had seized up, but they were half-clad or hardly clad at all.

Durkin and Calhoun came running from the post. They had pistols in their hands. They bawled questions that were not answered in the uproar. They followed the others toward the east gate. Beyond the stockade rifles began to explode as some of the guerrillas fired at shadows that they imagined were Apaches.

Mike made a dash to the rear of the frame buildings. He crawled beneath the two supply wagons which stood between the buildings and peered around a corner. The area was deserted. A man was standing in the open door of the lighted orderly room a few yards to Mike's left, but he, too, suddenly made up his mind and went racing to join the confused activity at the east end of the stockade.

Mike crawled to the door and peered in. The orderly room seemed to be deserted. A lantern hung from a peg, giving light. Ducking inside, he found that three rifles were stacked in a corner. A brace of pistols, holstered on belts, hung from a peg, along with ammunition pouches. An ammunition case stood open, containing canisters which contained powder cartridges.

Mike seized a blanket from a pallet in a corner, spread it on the floor and used it to form a bag in which he placed his booty.

Shouldering the load he peered from the door. His looting of the orderly room had taken only a minute or two and the vicinity was still clear of guerrillas.

He looked at the looming hoods of the supply wagons, struck by a new inspiration. He set his bundle down. Snatching the lantern from its peg, he shattered its globe with a blow against a post. He picked up the powder canister and ran out. Bursting paper cartridges, he scattered powder beneath the nearest wagon and dumped the contents of the canister upon it.

He shouldered the blanket again, backed off, and tossed the lantern with its open wick beneath the wagon. He turned and raced across the parade ground toward the rock house.

Powder flame gushed beneath the wagon. The stockade was brilliantly lighted and the guerrillas sighted him. They realized the truth. Bullets began to snap past him. One struck the muzzle of one of the rifles that projected from the shoulder pack. Its force spun him around, but he recovered and got into stride again.

A bullet tore the earth from beneath his foot when he was a stride or two from safety. Another struck him heavily in the thigh and he went down.

Guerrillas were racing toward him. Susan and Julia came from the door and dragged him with them. The three of them floundered through the door into the interior and fell in a heap.

Susan bounced to her feet and slammed the door. She crouched aside as bullets beat at the portal, chewing into the planks. Some tore entirely through the whipsawed post oak. The iron hinges held, but the planks were in danger of being torn from the crossbars.

139

Mike rolled to Susan, grasped her around the knees, dragging her off her feet. He hovered over her to shield her, for spent bullets were thudding against the rear walls.

He peered from a loophole. Guerrillas were only a dozen yards away, charging the house. Mike snatched a pistol from the heap of scattered booty and fired. He dropped a man with the first bullet. At the same moment Wheeler Fiske fired the rifle Mike had given him and another guerrilla was hit. That halted the rush. The guerrillas scattered for cover.

The wagons were burning fiercely. The mudwagon had caught fire also. The blaze was spreading to the frame buildings.

The guerrillas realized they faced a new problem. "Gawdamighty!" one screeched. "There goes our grub an' ammunition!"

"Get a bucket line going!" Calhoun shouted. "Hurry! Hurry!"

The guerrillas began a frantic search for pails in which to bring water from the spring. But what few containers they found were inadequate. Many of them, in increasing panic, came running with water in their hats in a ludicrous effort.

Both buildings were in flames. The heat drove the guerrillas back. The roof of the command post began to buckle.

"Drag the wagons to the spring!" Lew Durkin yelled. "Run 'em right into the spring! Hustle!"

One of the wagons erupted a massive pillar of flame. A sizable supply of powder had been touched off. The wagons and the coach were beyond saving and so were the buildings.

The glow of the fire reached through the openings in the windows, giving light enough to examine Mike's wound. The bullet had torn through the flesh just above the knee, inflicting an ugly gash that was forming a pool of blood on the floor. But it had missed the bone and had passed on through. Susan and Julia ripped strips from their clothing and bound the injury.

Mike tested the leg and found that he was able to hobble around on it. "One thing's for sure," he said. "We're going to look like scarecrows before long if we don't stop getting scraped and scratched and in need of bandaging."

"Here they come again!" Fiske warned.

Mike crawled to a firing position. Calhoun and Durkin, giving up hope of saving the wagons, had ordered the guerrillas to turn their attention back to the rock house. A ragged attack was being mounted. Men were advancing, but so cautiously that it was evident they had no real heart in it.

Mike and Fiske fired. Susan joined in, using one of the rifles Mike had rounded up. When the rifles were empty, Mike and Fiske opened up with the pistols.

At least one more of the guerrillas was hit. The others, outlined as they were by the glow of the fire, realized they would have to pay a high price to take the house and they broke, racing back to cover beyond the stockade walls. Mike could hear them bickering angrily with Durkin and Calhoun.

Presently they began firing at the house, concentrating on the windows and doors. Mike and his companions lay flat and escaped damage as slugs penetrated the planks and ricocheted in the room.

"Where did you learn to shoot and load a rifle?" he asked Susan.

"My father," she said.

"He must be a man of great forethought," Mike commented.

"I'll teach Julia how to load," she said.

The guerrilla Susan had slugged had regained consciousness. He was a source of danger to them if he worked free of his bonds. Mike released him, opened the door, and let him go running to rejoin his comrades.

Mike ducked from door to door, into the adjoining room where the women had been originally held. He made the leap before the guerrillas could draw a bead on him. Bullets stormed through the opening an instant too late.

He ripped planks from the bunk and table and pried away the chains and spiked planks from the door that connected the two rooms. He closed the two outer doors and wedged them shut. They could now move freely between the rooms and protect the entire perimeter of the house.

The structure stood fifty feet from the nearest wall of the stockade, which was to the north of them. That was the nearest shelter the guerrillas could find, and loopholes covered that approach also, with the fire lighting the area.

Mike moved around the building, shooting from one point and then another. Each report of the rifle brought an angry volley of bullets in return.

"Please stay still for a while," Susan protested. "You'll start your leg bleeding again."

Mike moved to another loophole and fired again. Once

more the weapons of the guerrillas burst into a fusillade.

It was Calhoun who caught onto his strategy. "Hold your fire, you idiots!" he yelled at his men. "They're only baiting you into wasting powder. We're in no——"

Calhoun bit it off in time. Mike was sure he had started to say that there was no powder to waste now that the wagons had burned.

On the other hand, the ammunition pouches Mike had seized in the orderly room were well filled. "We've got one edge on them at least," he told the others. "We can keep shooting longer."

CHAPTER SEVENTEEN

The shooting ended. Mike was unable to draw a reply when he fired from various points, and he gave it up.

"They've got no way of knowing about Dean getting away," he said to Susan. "They likely figure it might be that way, but they can't be sure. They might take it for granted that the horse he got away on just stampeded into the hills with the rest of the stock. They really aren't sure just how strong we are."

"Are you sure he *did* get away?" Susan asked anxiously.

"About the only thing that can happen to him is if his horse steps in a gopher hole and he gets his confounded neck busted," Mike said.

"Apparently you'd be happy if that happened."

"If we get out of this jackpot," Mike said, "I've got a few things to say to him—with fists."

"Look!" Julia exclaimed, peering from a window. "They're going to try to burn us out!"

Guerrillas beyond the north wall were igniting wads of dry grass and leaves which they were tossing toward the roof. The majority of the firewads fell short or bounced harmlessly off the roof. Those that did remain ignited the dry weeds and grass from last year's crop that had grown on the roof. When these were burned off, the foot-thick layer of earth remained impervious.

The guerrillas finally gave it up as a waste of effort. A comparative silence came again.

"Whoever the army officer was who built this place," Susan said, "will get a big smacking kiss if I ever run across him."

"Two smackers," Julia said.

They were trying to make a stab at being lighthearted. But they knew that Kirby Dean might have met up with difficulties far greater than gopher holes. Apaches, for one. At best, the information Fiske had as to the whereabouts of the supposed Union force was sketchy. And its existence might be legendary.

Mike wondered how long the guerrillas would bide their time. Probably they were waiting until the glow of the fire died down so that it would no longer make targets of them. Clouds had sailed in over the high ridges to the west, and the moon was already hidden. The basin would be in total darkness when the embers of the buildings faded.

Fiske's thoughts were running along the same line. "They'll probably rush us before daybreak," he murmured to Mike. "They can come in and take us if they really carry it through."

"That's exactly the point," Mike said. "Would they sustain a rush? They've got to come through those two doors. These rifles are Maynards. They're rated at penetrating four inches of pine wood at a hundred yards. The Enfield is just as good. Then there are three six-shooters. One rifle bullet would tear through two or three of them at point-blank range. We could pile them up in the doors. They know that. It's my belief they won't try it that way. They'll try to outlast us."

"But with their food gone and their ammunition about——"

"They'll stick," Mike said. "After all, there's a hundred and fifty thousand dollars waiting for them. And if they get the money it means looting San Francisco in the bargain. As for food, horse meat isn't such bad fare. I've been on horse-meat ration a time or two. They'll round up the stampeded stock after daybreak. They've got something else that we haven't got. Water."

Nobody said anything for a space. There was no further attempt at levity.

Fiske took Julia's hand. "It's simple enough, dear," he said. "Tell me where you hid that infernal money. I'll lead them to it on condition, of course, that the rest of you are allowed to go on your way."

Julia leaned close and kissed him on the cheek. "There isn't any money any longer, Wheeler," she said.

"What do you mean?" Wheeler asked.

"It's gone," she said. "All of it. Money and papers. Burned." Their expressions caused her to smile wanly. "It was in the buildings that burned," she said.

"Will you say that again?" Mike exclaimed.

"The money was in Calhoun's trunk," she said.

"Calhoun's?"

"Yes. I had decided that he was after the money and that this Bill Jackson-Lew Durkin person was in on it too. I hid it

144

in Calhoun's baggage because I was at my wit's end and that seemed to me about the last place they would look—at least until he reached his destination. I saw them carry the baggage from the mudwagon into those buildings after they locked us up in this place. It must still have been there."

"But I searched Calhoun's trunk at Fort Yuma!" Susan exclaimed. "And yours."

"I put the petticoat in it only the other night while we were struggling over the old trail," Julia explained. "I slipped it off during one of the times when the baggage was unloaded to lighten the coach. The rest of you were busy helping get the coach over a washout. I stuffed the petticoat in the bottom of the trunk beneath the clothes that were packed there."

She looked at Fiske. "I'm sorry, Wheeler. So sorry."

Fiske walked to the bunk and sank down. His arm was swollen around the blood-caked bandage. He was shockingly haggard, his eyes hot, but sunken. For him a great dream was finally smashed.

Julia spoke again, her voice dead with her grief for him. "I thought it might get the money through to Texas. It looked like the only way. It all went wrong."

Fiske managed a smile for her, pulling it from the bitter depths of his defeat. "Of course, dear. It's all right. But this doesn't change anything. Calhoun doesn't know the money's gone. We'll do as I said."

"You'll lead him into the hills on a wild-goose chase," Mike said. "And when you can't show him any money you know what'll happen to you, don't you? Ever been hung up by the heels over a fire?"

"It will buy time," Fiske said. He looked at his swollen arm. "And my time is limited."

He looked around at them appealingly. "A day, perhaps, is all we need. Dean will come back—with help. I believe that. I have faith in it."

Mike shook his head. "We'll all hang and rattle here together."

Fiske was too spent to debate it. He sank back on the bunk, closing his eyes. But Mike felt that he had not changed his views.

The burned buildings had fallen into heaps of embers which the wind stirred at times into flames. The heat reached their stronghold. The rock walls were hot. The air inside grew stifling. They lay flat on the floor where breathing was more endurable.

The guerrillas made two more demonstrations before morning, but these were mere feints that faded when Mike and the two young women fired a few shots from loopholes.

"They're trying to wear us down physically," Fiske said.

"And goad us into using up powder," Mike said.

Mike's thirst was an agony. His tongue was swelling. His wound throbbed and his skin was dry with fever.

Susan moved to his side at the loophole where he sat. "Get some sleep," she said. "You're our only salvation. Our only strength. Julia and I will stay awake. Rest while you can."

She placed an arm around him and drew his head onto her shoulder. Mike pressed his dry lips against her throat. He felt her lips against his temple. He slept in her arms.

At times he would start up, reaching for his rifle, dreaming that the guerrillas were coming. The moon was gone and the embers of the buildings cast little light. But the guerrillas, not realizing how weak the defense had become, made no attack. Each time he fell asleep again, Susan at his side.

Daybreak came. He emerged from the drugging weakness. His leg, he decided, was at least no worse beneath its stiffened bandage.

Susan smiled gravely at him. She stretched face down on the floor, pillowing her head on her arms, and was instantly asleep. Julia moved to her side and they slept, clasping hands for mutual comfort.

Water was now their torturing need, but Fiske's plight was the worst. His arm was frightfully swollen. His face was the color of dry slate. The sun came up and blazed down as the morning advanced. A sluggish breeze began drawing down the flat and brought the heat of the smoldering ashes upon the building, adding to their ordeal.

At times the guerrillas would fire a few shots and pretend to mount an attack. But, like those of the night, these ended at the first sign of rifle muzzles at the loopholes.

It was a siege. The guerrillas evidently had decided that time was on their side and there was no point in exposing themselves by open assault. They controlled the spring and they were sure that this was the weapon that would inevitably prevail. Mike believed they were right.

The guerrillas made the most of their advantage. Water was poured over the stockade walls, wasting itself in the soil. Mike and his companions watched the water spill down. They could hear its tantalizing gurgle and splash. It was pure torture.

Fiske was breathing unevenly. His shattered arm was sapping away his life. Julia stayed at his side constantly.

Suddenly she lifted her voice. "Calhoun!" she called. "Vance! Can you hear me?"

"Very plainly, Julia," Calhoun replied.

"Give us water and bandages!" she said. "Wheeler will die unless——"

Mike reached her side and placed a hand over her mouth, silencing her. "That's what they want to hear," he said. "Don't tell them anything! Nothing!"

Calhoun was answering. "Certainly, Julia. We've got plenty of water. And medicine for Wheeler. Come out and get them. Come yourself, and we'll talk it over."

"Why can't I tell them the money's burned?" she breathed hysterically. "They'll go away then."

"They won't believe it," Mike said. "They'll try to force you to talk. And they'll only take it out on you when they find out you're telling the truth."

"I can't believe that," she sobbed. "Calhoun can't be that brutal."

"He can be," Mike said. "Remember Murdock."

"Yes," she said. "Yes. I remember."

Susan placed an arm around her, consoling her.

The siege went on.

Mike spent the greater part of the time at the small window in the east wall, peering between slits in the planks.

Susan finally spoke. "What is it, Mike? What are you watching?"

"I can see down the flat through a gap out onto the open country eastward," Mike said. "I thought I spotted dust above the sand hills a long way out there this morning. It was shining in the sun. There was no wind at the time—at least up here."

They aroused, suddenly galvanized by hope. "Horses!" Julia exclaimed. "Riders! Dean *did* find——"

"It could only have been a whirlie," Mike said. "The wind might have been blowing down there. It faded out and that was the last of it."

He saw them sink back into apathy.

The guerrillas became active late in the afternoon. They were gathering brush in the hills and dragging it near the stockade walls.

Julia was sleeping. Fiske lay in a stupor. Susan had said nothing for a long time. Finally she moved close to Mike's side and leaned against him. "It's about over with," she murmured. "It *was* only the wind that made the dust this morning."

He held her close against him. It was plain enough. The guerrillas, after dark and before moonrise, would have no difficulty in tossing the dry brush over the walls and heaping it against the rock house. It would burn fiercely and wrap them in unbearable heat. They would have to surrender.

"If it comes to that," Mike said, "you stay with Julia. They won't harm her as long as they believe she can lead them to the money."

"I'll stay with you," Susan said.

"No, no," Mike said desperately. "Julia can win time for both of you. That'll do the trick. You'll see Kirby Dean again."

Her eyes were suddenly swimming with tears, but she was trying to smile up at him. "McLish—McLish! Can't you see *anything*? Don't you understand that Dean is my brother?"

His expression brought a warm little sigh of anguish from her. "You were so righteous in your suspicion of me and of Dean," she sobbed. "So sure that we were in this only for ourselves. I was angry with you. I wouldn't let Dean tell you the truth. His real name is Dean Vickers. I'm Susan Vickers. Roger Vickers is our father."

He could only look at her. All the futility, all the emptiness was gone from him. There was still much to be explained, but all the questions that had really baffled him were suddenly answered.

He kissed her—tentatively at first, questioningly. Then with a vast knowledge of what this meant, as her arms tightened around him. He was thinking that he should have known this long ago. The resemblance was there. Much of Roger Vickers was in both of them.

"A hell of a time to find this out," he said huskily.

She clung to him for a long time. The crashing of brush being tossed over the stockade wall came to them. She shivered and drew away.

The sun had left the flat. The light had faded in their stronghold, leaving them in gloom. And it was a stronghold no longer.

Julia and Fiske awakened. "What is it?" Julia cried.

Mike had no answer. Julia rushed to a loophole and gazed. The hope went out of her. She moved to Fiske's side and took his hand.

Mike fired occasionally at guerrillas, but they were fleeting targets and it was only a waste of powder.

Dusk deepened and the guerrillas moved with greater boldness. The stars came out. Guerrillas were inside the walls in numbers now, pushing stacks of dry brush against the north wall of the house. Concealed by the bulk of the fuel, they jeered the defenders. The mass of brush finally reached to the roof.

Lew Durkin spoke near at hand. "You, in there! You, McLish and the rest of you! I've got flint and steel in my hand and gunpower to start this stuff going. It'll burn fast and hot. I'll give you sixty seconds to make up your minds. Throw your guns out first, then come onto the parade ground, your hands in the air. All of you! Dean, Fiske, the women! Every one of you. If so, I won't flint this powder. But whether you come out peaceful or not, you're coming out."

Durkin had disclosed that he believed Kirby Dean was still in the house with them. That explained why the guerrillas had waited out the day rather than risk a frontal attack.

Mike hid a pistol in the tatters of his shirt. "I'm coming out!" he shouted. "I'll take you to the money after the others are on their way out of this."

He lost the final try to win more time. "I've had enough stalling!" Durkin roared. "Come out, all of you, or roast! And when you do come out, that woman will tell the truth or I'll put a hot iron to her."

Mike heard the cold hiss of ignited gunpowder as Durkin struck flint with steel. "Get ready!" he said. "I'll go out first. Stay back of me."

His thought now was that he might be able to take Durkin or Calhoun with him, for he knew they intended to shoot him down on sight. Perhaps he might get both of them. That, at least, would cause confusion among the guerrillas and would perhaps gain time for the others.

He helped Fiske to his feet. They gripped hands. "I'm sorry I got you and Miss Lang into this, McLish," Fiske said. "So very sorry."

Susan came to Mike and kissed him. "I waited too long," she murmured drearily. "Now there's no time to be happy together."

Mike heard it then—the first shot in the distance. And the yelling. More shooting. It grew in volume. He could hear the clatter of galloping horses.

The brush began to roar against the wall of the house as the blaze took hold. Flames appeared at the window.

Mike freed the door and they crouched there, peering out. Guns were exploding beyond the stockade. The guerrillas were scattering. They were retreating past the rock house. Many were trying to ram fresh charges into their rifles.

Riders appeared outside the walls. Dusty men. The glow of the blazing brush reached them. Soldiers were there. Union soldiers, their uniforms so faded and stained there was little to distinguish them from others who were civilians. These were stagecoach men, Mike realized.

He seized Susan in a wild bear hug. "Your brother didn't pile up in a gopher hole after all! He found the Butterfield outfit!"

Susan began to laugh and sob hysterically. "It *was* more than dust you saw this morning!" she babbled. "More than dust!"

Riders poured through the east gate, pursuing the retreating guerrillas. One of the arrivals spurred his lathered horse toward the rock house. He was Dean—Dean Vickers.

He swung to the ground and said hoarsely, "Thank God, you're all alive!"

It was Julia he seized in his arms. He held her as though he never wanted to let her go.

The guerrillas were attempting to use the west wall of the stockade as a breastworks. Mike saw Durkin and Calhoun racing among them, trying to organize them.

Mike began hobbling in that direction. The fight could still be lost, for the guerrillas had the numbers and the strength to stand off tired attackers, once they rallied in a strong position.

"Durkin!" Mike shouted. The guerrilla leader heard that through the tumult and whirled.

He had pistols in his hands. Calhoun, a few yards from him, also turned, weapons poised.

"Durkin!" Mike said again. He and Durkin fired at each other, the reports blending in a heavy concussion.

Mike felt Durkin's bullet rake along the base of his neck. He fired again but the shot was not needed. Durkin was reeling, his body contorted as though he had been skewered. Mike's bullet had torn through his chest—a death blow.

Calhoun fired before Mike could veer his weapon in that direction. But the bullet had not been meant for him.

A few paces away another pistol had come into action. It exploded a second time and a third.

Each slug was finding Calhoun, the impacts a savage sound. He fell and convulsively touched off his two pistols again, the reports blowing a great cloud of dust from the dry earth into which the muzzles were pointed.

It was Dean Vickers who had slain Calhoun. And it had been Dean at whom Calhoun had fired—and missed.

The guerrillas, with no leaders to inspire them, continued their demoralized flight. They abandoned the fort and tried to scatter into cover in the brush beyond.

They were easy pickings for the cavalrymen who rode them down with sabers whirling. Within minutes it was all over. The survivors quit, throwing away their arms and shouting surrender.

Mike explored the wound on his neck. Some blood was flowing, but he decided that it was no more than a crease.

He and Dean walked to where Calhoun and Durkin lay. For Durkin, Mike had no feeling. During all his life the man had gambled that this day would never arrive for him. It was inevitable that he would eventually lose.

He felt a measure of pity for Calhoun. His handsome face was set in a grimace. His body lay twisted, torn by bullets, stained with the blood that would never flow again. Insects were already gathering.

Mike looked at Dean and said, "That shooting was at more than thirty paces. I'd say about forty. Where did you learn to handle a gun?"

"In the army," Dean said. "I'm a lieutenant, West Point class of '58, detached for special duty at the request of my father. My real name is—"

"I know your name," Mike said. "And damn your soul for letting me sweat so long."

"It was Sue's idea," Dean grinned. "She's the one who sweated you. She had her nose bent because she thought you'd fallen for Julia. She wanted your scalp for herself."

"She's got it," Mike said. "And I'm a happy man."

"God help you," Dean said. "She'll lead you a merry life, but I believe you're tough enough to keep the upper hand."

They walked back to the rock house. The captain of the cavalry detachment rode up and slid stiffly down. "Your friends seem to be still all in one piece, mister," he said to Dean.

"They are," Dean said. "This is my sister, Sue. And Mike McLish. And this is Miss Julia Fortune and Mr. Wheeler Fiske."

The captain touched his hat and said, "Miss Sue. Miss Fortune. A great pleasure. Comely ladies are a novelty in these parts. Indeed they are."

He shook hands with Mike. He was curt to Fiske. "Vickers has told me about you, Mr. Fiske," he said. "I must say that I don't know exactly how to regard you. I wonder if I have the authority to put you under arrest. The trouble is the country's full of men like you. It'll all likely be decided peaceful."

Julia spoke quickly. "What Mr. Fiske needs is a doctor. And water and rest."

The officer looked at her and softened. "Of course, ma'am. We'll do what we can. We've no doctor with us, but there's a man with the civilians who's had medical experience."

"How soon—?" Julia began.

"The civilian column won't overtake us until tomorrow," the captain said. "I'll send for the man to come up tonight, if possible."

Mike cornered Susan alone at first chance. "So you made me sweat!" he said. "Dean made a full confession."

"You deserved it," she sniffed. "Making eyes at Julia. Putting your arm around her."

"Never mind that," Mike said. "There are things that need explaining. How did you and Dean get into this in the first place?"

"Dean and I had lived in the East the biggest part of the time," she said. "We were educated there. We lived there with relatives after Mother died. That was when we were half-grown. Dean graduated from West Point. I was sent to finishing school. Our faces weren't too well known in San Francisco, particularly since we grew up. So Dad, who was at his wit's end to find someone he could trust, sent for us to help him in this thing against Mr. Fiske. Dean was given leave from the Army. He was supposed to pose as a secessionist and stay in San Francisco to try to find out who were backing Mr. Fiske. But Dad had to send him on this trip when——"

"When I stood on my scruples," Mike said.

Susan was looking at Dean Vickers and Julia, who had walked away and were standing alone. They were not talking.

Julia had a hand on Dean's arm. They merely stood close to each other.

Mike said, "What's going to become of them?"

Neither of them had an answer for that. For it was in the attitudes of both Dean and Julia that they knew that for them there would soon be a parting.

It was nearly a week later when Mike, sitting in a stage-coach, which moved along with a sizable column, looked back as the stockade walls of Fort Fortymile began to fall behind.

The column included some twoscore of Concords, mud-wagons, and supply wagons which had been seized by Union loyalists when the Butterfield line had been abandoned east of the Chiricahuas.

Agents sent by Butterfield interests on the same mission on which Alexander Majors had sent Mike, rode with the column. There had been many defections. Stock and coaches had been seized by Southern men, and were now well on their way to Texas. But Central Overland would be the major gainer in the breakup.

Fiske, pale and drawn, but well on the mend, sat in the rear seat with Julia at his side. Constant care by Julia and Susan had brought him back from the brink of death. His arm had been saved.

Once again Susan sat between Mike and her brother in the forward seat. The ghosts of Calhoun and Lew Durkin, who lay buried at Fort Fortymile, now rode with them.

It was perhaps these ghosts that brought the constraint that held them now. Susan's hand rested on Mike's arm. Between them was a deep content. But Dean Vickers and Julia rode in silence. For Fiske sat stern and unyielding, his beliefs and his determination unchanged. And Julia, although she had never again put it in words, would never turn against him.

The parting was upon them sooner than they had antici-pated. The column halted, with Fort Fortymile still in sight in the morning sun to the east.

Mike looked out. Moving down the trail from the west came another column. This one consisted of nondescript wagons, but had no stagecoaches in line. The loose stock that was being driven along included milk cows, goats, mules and donkeys. There were even turkeys being marched

153

along, guarded by children. Chickens squawked in wagon crates.

The Union captain came riding by and pulled up alongside to speak to Mike and Dean. "More of the damned secess," he said, half admiringly. "They're getting out of California and heading for Dixie. Likely, if it comes to a shooting war, some of 'em'll be drawing a bead on the likes of people like us."

He added, "But there's nothing I can do about it. After all, there's been no war declared. And I reckon there never will be. Imagine, fighting with your own kind."

Julia leaned forward suddenly. She kissed Dean Vickers. She clung to him and began to weep. She wept as Mike had never heard a woman weep.

"Someday!" she sobbed. "Oh, someday, my darling!"

Dean, white-faced, did not attempt to hold her when she drew away. All he did was to look at Fiske and say, "Damn you and your pride. Damn your beliefs."

Fiske did not answer. He let Julia help him from the coach to join the eastbound column. He stood there a moment looking up at them.

"This is the way it must always be," he said. "A man must fight for his beliefs. How else would there be any pride in living? How else would a man be free? It has to be this way. Men's pride is the burden of women. They have to wait."

He looked at Dean. "And Julia will wait. I know her. You two will meet again. I have faith that you will."

He walked away from the coach to meet the oncoming column from the west. He leaned on Julia's arm. She looked back only once at Dean. "Yes," she said. "I'll wait for you."

Susan leaned against Mike and began to weep. She did not try to comfort her brother. This was not the time to shake a man's resolution.

First Lieutenant Dean Vickers, of the Army of the United States of America, had orders to report for duty at Washington as soon as his special mission was completed. The order was signed by General Winfield Scott, commander in chief.

His mission was now completed.

"There'll be no war," Mike said confidently. "You'll see her again, and soon. And get married. Speaking of things like that, you've got another little chore ahead of you. We'll need a best man when we hit San Francisco. Your father, of course, will give away the bride."

The Butterfield column moved ahead again, rigidly ignoring the eastbound wagons which veered off the trail and passed by a few hundred yards to the south.

Susan continued to weep. It was the way of women to look on the dark side of things. Mike knew that she did not share the opinion he voiced. The truth was that, in his heart, he no longer believed it himself. War was coming and she knew that he too would be in it.

He drew from his pocket the star he had found in the shabby house. It had grown more tattered, and bore the stain of blood. He gave it to Susan for safekeeping.

He looked back. The gray boulders that had been rolled into place to mark the graves of Calhoun and Durkin were still visible on the barren slope overlooking Fort Fortymile. Soon these too were lost in the shimmering distance.